The Big Cover-Up

Also by Daphne Ledward and published by Robson Books

SIMPLY GARDENING

THE AWKWARD SPOT

The Big Cover-Up

All You Need to Know about Ground Cover

Daphne Ledward

Robson Books

> ERRATA
> The captions for the photographs that appear on pages 87 and 88 are to be found on page 91, not page 86. Those for pages 89 and 90 are to be found on pages 106 and 109 and those for pages 107 and 108 are on page 86.

Colour photographs by John Hands
Line drawings by Chris Olney

First published in Great Britain in 1989 by Robson Books Ltd, Bolsover House, 5–6 Clipstone Street, London W1P 7EB.

Copyright © 1989 Daphne Ledward

British Library Cataloguing in Publication Data
Ledward, Daphne
  The Big Cover-Up.
  1. Gardens. Ground coverplants
  I. Title
  635.9'64

ISBN 0 86051 559 1

All rights reserved. No part of this publication may be reproduced, stored in a retrieval system, or transmitted in any form or by any means, electronic, mechanical, photocopying, recording or otherwise, without the prior permission in writing of the publishers.

Printed in Great Britain by St Edmundsbury Press Ltd, Bury St Edmunds, Suffolk.

Contents

Acknowledgements	6
Introduction	7
Ground cover for large, open areas	18
Ground cover for partially shaded areas, including dappled shade under trees	53
Ground cover for heavy shade	75
Ground cover to bind loose earth	82
Ground cover in rose beds	96
Roses as ground cover	103
Using climbers as ground cover	113
Taller shrubs as ground cover	123
Useful Addresses and Bibliography	141

Acknowledgements

I would like to thank Johnson's Seeds of Boston, Lincolnshire, and Notcutts Garden Centre, Peterborough, for allowing me the freedom of their trial and display grounds.

Introduction

Ground Cover – myth or magic?
There are three kinds of people who own gardens. First, there are those who derive great pleasure from the occupation, and do not mind how difficult they make life for themselves in their pursuit of total satisfaction. The second division does not see a lot of fun in slaving all day over a hot spade, but is prepared to admit it *is* rather nice to relax on the lounger sipping a cold gin and tonic and surrounded by well-thought-out, well-cared-for herbage. The third type of person quite unashamedly loathes gardens, gardening and anything remotely connected with it, and is fortunate enough to be able to turn a totally blind eye to the wilderness that greets him (or her) every time they step outside the home.

This book is aimed at the second category, the people who want a good effect with what is hoped to be the minimum amount of effort. Somewhere they have heard about this magical form of planting – ground-cover – which, after the initial effort of planting, will enable them to enjoy beautiful surroundings without hard work ever after.

Unfortunately the reality is not quite so simple.

The delights and disappointments of ground-cover
There are many prospective gardeners who seem to have a mental image of 'ground-cover' plants as mysterious species, capable of exuding some sort of magical substance which banishes weeds for ever. Not only that, but they see them as 'superplants', requiring, once planted, neither feeding, watering, pruning nor any other form of maintenance whatever. It is these misconceptions which cause so much disappointment and frustration.

There is no peculiarity unique to plants commonly recommended for ground-cover purposes which is not found in nearly every form of vegetation. If you think about it, *all* plants cover the ground to some extent! The principle behind ground-cover planting is that unwanted colonization of an area is very difficult if light is excluded from the ground. For example, you will find few plants growing under a mature shrub, densely branched conifer or large tree. The species capable of thriving in such conditions are quite limited, and because germinating seedlings need light and moisture once a shoot has been produced in order to become strongly established, it is unlikely that many young weeds will get a strong hold. The thicker the branches or the closer the planting, the harder it is for unwelcome 'visitors' to survive. So in a ground-cover scheme all that happens is that this principle is taken a step further, by planting much closer than the normal spacing for whatever species is being used, in order to keep as much light as possible off the ground and also to ensure that there is little room for weed development should any manage to invade the area.

Once established for a year or two, ground-cover schemes are undeniably a blessing. Weeding is reduced quite considerably, and if large quantities of single species are used, pruning and other routine maintenance jobs are made much easier as you are doing the same things to the same plants at the same time. Mass plantings generally look good, too, as you get the full benefit of the foliage, flowering or even bark effect.

Disappointment starts to creep in, however, if the fact that ground-cover plants are simply garden plants used in a slightly different way, and, as such, are likely to require the same attention and have the same 'hang-ups' as those in the shrubbery or herbaceous border, is not fully appreciated. They are bought as small, young specimens, and however closely you position them (there is usually an optimum distance anyway and closer spacing will not be any more effective in the long run – it may even be detrimental) there will be a period during their formative years when they won't cover the ground, and so will have to be weeded in just the normal way until they provide enough of a canopy to start doing the job intended.

A less backbreaking way of keeping down weeds is to use a total weedkiller, which must be recommended for application around plants. Simazine and Casoron G4 are both suitable for use around shrubs if applied strictly according to the manufacturer's instructions, but at the time of writing there is nothing available to the amateur gardener which will control weeds in herbaceous plants. Weedkillers applied as a liquid, like simazine, are more difficult to apply than granular ones – Casoron G4, for example – as there is always the danger of drift onto the foliage of the plants you do not want to kill.

INTRODUCTION

It goes without saying, however, that whether you are using a liquid or a granular herbicide, it should only be applied when there is not a breath of wind. For the longest effect, these weedkillers should be applied in early spring, preferably to weed-free soil. You should then be able to expect up to twelve months of satisfactory weed control.

A newer way of preventing weed growth which is being used increasingly in very large public schemes is to spread a mulch of chipped bark. If this is put on to a depth of no less than 2 inches (5cm) it should prevent weed growth for up to three years. It will not eliminate well-established, tough perennial weeds, though, so it is wise, again, to apply the mulch to weed-free soil.

Bark chippings can also have drawbacks. One of the main problems is that birds seem to take an evil delight in throwing them everywhere, which not only makes the average-sized garden look untidy, but can also play havoc with the mower blades. A more scientific disadvantage is that, as the chips start to rot down, they tend to rob the soil of nitrogen in order for the bacteria involved to function properly. At a time when you are wanting the young plants to put on as much growth as possible to provide good coverage, nitrogen shortage is just what you do *not* want, so it must be supplied in the form of a high-nitrogen fertilizer in early summer. This, in turn, accelerates the rotting process, necessitating another application of mulch earlier than usual, which you do not particularly want either, and so on.

There is also a school of thought which says that bark chips – which are, essentially, pieces of dead wood – can introduce a very serious fungal disease. Armillaria, otherwise known as bootlace or honey fungus, feeds off dead wood, but invades live woody tissue also, and it is both fatal and impossible to treat. However, this risk can be reduced by using a proprietary brand like 'Cambark', which has been specially processed to minimize the possibility of fungal disease appearing.

Ground-cover planting is all about keeping weeds down, so it is important that the land should be thoroughly cleaned of all perennial weeds before you can even start to think about planting up. There is no way that this kind of planting, even when mature, will be able to deal in entirety with species like horsetail, couch grass, ground elder, horseradish and docks, all of which are extremely difficult to eradicate.

THE BIG COVER-UP

You may find that these weeds are impossible even to dig out, in which case the only answer is to allow a good coverage of weeds to grow up and then treat them with a herbicide like 'Tumbleweed', which contains the chemical glyphosate. This is absorbed by the leaves and is taken down to the roots over a period of 1–4 weeks. When the top growth is completely dead – and not before – the ground can be dug over, as most of the weeds will have been killed completely, though you may get some regrowth if they are really well-established, and this must be treated again before introducing the new plants. One thing is certain, however – you will be wasting both your time and money if you do not clean your weeds up thoroughly. I have so often seen ground-cover plantings which should have been excellent, but were, in fact, a total disaster because the preliminaries were skimped.

Another misconception is that, just because the most commonly recommended subjects are obligingly robust, there is less need to take care with their actual planting. Unfortunately, I cannot give you an excuse to short-cut this job either! As in every other field of gardening, plants cannot be expected to grow away rapidly and thrive for many years if all the attention they received on planting was for a hole to be drilled in a rock-hard piece of earth and the root ball stuffed in – and never mind if the hole is a bit small, just push harder!

The site must be properly dug, and if the soil is poor – very sandy or full of clay – you should incorporate as much organic matter as you can lay your hands on: peat, garden compost, spent mushroom compost, farmyard manure and the like. Adding a general purpose compound fertilizer like 'Vitax Q4', 'Enmag' or even growmore a week or so before planting will be beneficial. Although containerization has made it theoretically possible to plant up all the year round, there are still many advantages to be gained by planting in late October and November, when the soil is still warm enough to get the roots away to a good start, but while the plants themselves are in their resting period.

If the site has been properly prepared, there should be no difficulty in digging good-sized holes and giving each specimen personal attention. Of course, it does seem a daunting task when faced with dozens, or even hundreds, of little black pots, but because the object of the exercise is to save labour in the long run, it really is worth devoting a little more time and effort to the scheme at this stage.

INTRODUCTION

The aftercare of plants used in this way should be exactly the same as if they were planted in a normal border. New arrivals will obviously need much more attention than plants which have been growing well for a number of years. The type of care will vary somewhat according to species, but it is a safe bet that, after weeding, the most time-consuming task will be watering in dry spells. To ensure that the individual plants join up as quickly as possible, they should never receive a check to growth, so they must not dry out. This is where a mulch, put down on top of thoroughly moist soil, can be helpful.

It is unlikely that any pruning will be necessary for some time, but a periodic tidying of the bed and the individual plants is desirable. Also, if herbaceous forms are used – of which more later – there will have to be some cutting down and removal of dead leaves at the end of the year. However, once the planting begins to mature, there may well have to be some pruning from time to time, though the amount and the form it will take again will depend largely on the species used.

A close planting of this kind will, of course, require feeding to keep it growing strongly, as vast amounts of nutrients will be taken from the soil. Fertilizing is not difficult when the plants are young, as there is plenty of ground in between into which the food can be worked. The fertilizers suggested on page 10 are suitable for an annual top dressing in spring, and bonemeal can be applied in autumn every second year to encourage good root formation.

The difficulty with feeding comes when there is a lot of top growth. It is not a good idea to throw the plant food all over the foliage; very little of it will actually reach the roots and the concentrated powder or granules will probably damage the leaves. One way round the problem is to liquid feed at regular intervals throughout the summer, using a hose-end diluter if the area is very large. Liquid fertilizer does not remain in the soil as long as powder or granules, and so it is necessary to spend much more time on the job if the plants are to receive adequate nourishment. The only answer if you prefer to feed dry is to lift up all the top growth and spread the fertilizer on the soil beneath, hoe it in as much as possible, and then water well to start it getting into solution. It is usually pretty dry under a mature ground-cover planting and if water is not added immediately, the fertilizer can sit there, quite useless, for months. This form of dry feeding is not recommended for very prickly subjects unless you are prepared to wear a suit of armour!

Choosing the right plants for the job

Having already said that virtually any plant is ground cover, I will probably have thrown everyone into utter confusion as I destroy their preconceived ideas about suitable species, as likely as not gained from a glossy catalogue or that over-optimistic weekend newspaper advertisement which generally begins, 'END THE DRUDGERY OF WEEDING FOREVER' and goes on to hint seductively about 'miracle plants'.

The most effective way of choosing varieties for mass planting is to consider what you are trying to achieve and then think about the habits of the plants you feel might fit the bill. Somewhere along the line, unfortunately, cost might have to come into it. The reason why certain plants are so popular as ground cover is not so much the way they do the job, but the fact that they can be propagated easily and inexpensively in vast numbers and therefore are less likely to bankrupt the garden-owner.

The first essential is that the candidate must be capable of excluding light from the soil around it when it is mature. This will eliminate plants with widely spaced branches and very fine or filigree leaves, but it need not prevent the use of deciduous types, or even herbaceous species which die down completely in winter, because it is during the summer months that weeds are most inclined to grow.

The ideal ground-cover plant should have a dense branch structure or thick, profuse or large leaf habit. Most ground-cover suggestions favour ground-hugging plants or those of low-growing tendencies, but it is not vital that they should grow close to the ground; many of the most satisfactory schemes involve shrubs and even herbaceous perennials which are considerably taller, providing the canopy obscures plenty of light from the ground beneath.

A good ground-cover subject should also be strong and quick-growing, and suitable for the position it is intended for. Many shrubs would make excellent ground-cover plants given the time, but the whole idea is that the scheme should reach the low-maintenance stage as quickly as possible, which eliminates all slow-growing species (these also are unlikely to be practical on cost grounds alone). Nor are plants which do not do particularly well in your area very desirable; the very last thing you want to have to do is pamper something which

INTRODUCTION

ultimately should be pampering you!

A typical example of this is the use of the wild rhododendron, *Rhododendron ponticum*. In an acid soil, given a moist, semi-shaded woodland situation, it makes first-rate ground cover. In hot, limey sites it would soon begin to look pretty sick, and yet I have often seen it recommended in advertisements as being an ideal ground-cover shrub, without any mention being made as to its preferences. Wherever possible in this book I have tried to describe only species which should do well in any soil, but of course whether the site is in sun or shade has to have a bearing on the selection of varieties.

Low-growing ground-cover plants – and some taller ones, too – frequently cover the soil not only with their spreading branches, but also by their ability to propagate themselves *in situ*, thus increasing the density of the planting stations. Many forms of cotoneaster and euonymous produce roots at the nodes where they touch the soil, soon making an impenetrable thicket. *Hypericum calycinum* and some forms of spiraea, symphoricarpus (snowberry) and cornus have a suckering (runner-producing) habit which ensures that individual specimens soon join up and become intermingled.

Another prerequisite for a ground-cover subject is that it must be long-lived. Some of the most efficient schemes have taken many years to establish. It is useless to consider a massed planting of, say, lupins, which have a notoriously short life-span (although in good soils they will self-seed if not dead-headed) or brooms, which can also be a bit temperamental. On the other hand, many good shrubs can have an expected life of several decades. One could, I suppose, class the massed bedding schemes of spring and summer flowering annuals as ground cover – when they are planted thickly and in full growth not many weeds stand a chance – but they can hardly be called 'long-lived', or labour-saving, for that matter!

The plants selected for use on a bank must have certain attributes. The most useful ones are those which bind the soil as well as covering it. Shrubs which sucker, have extensive root systems or root themselves where the branches touch the soil are the best. If the bank receives a lot of wind it is probably better to use low-growing plants, as some taller shrubs can loosen or blow right out.

Above all, plants should be frost-hardy under normal winter conditions. A ground-cover scheme which has to be replaced after every cold snap is pointless, although after some of the abnormally

THE BIG COVER-UP

severe winters of the late 1970s and 1980s, temporary damage was seen to occur on shrubs generally thought of as fully hardy. In most cases there was a full recovery during the following summer after some trimming back.

If there is a possibility of damage, for example from vandals, weather, animals or children, use plants with a capacity for quick recovery. Initial cost must be of paramount importance here, as the chances are you may have to replace some of the plants in the early stages.

Where you intend to cover a large area, a better effect can be achieved by using several toning or contrasting species rather than just one. While you often see the latter on large tracts of public land, for example road embankments and central reservations, the same idea in a domestic garden generally gives a rather monotonous appearance. Instead of using, for instance, large quantities of *Euonymus radicans* 'Variegatus', you could try dividing the quantity into three, and use other forms of euonymus as well, like *E.r.* 'Emerald 'n Gold', and *E.r.* 'Gold Tip'. They are all plants of similar habit, with variegated leaves, but the colour of the variegation is different in each case, so you get toning and shading instead of a wall or blanket of one shade of green.

If you intend to use a subject where the attraction depends largely on its flowers, you might prefer a mass of a single species to give a greater spectacle. The effect you get if you contrast a very dark-leaved shrub like *Cotoneaster dammeri* with a very light-leaved one, like the grey *Hebe pagei* or the golden *Spiraea* 'Golden Princess' may be to your liking or it may not, depending on whether you prefer brashness or subtlety, but such combinations are not 'wrong', whatever anyone may say! If it is your garden, you like the effect, and you are paying for it, good luck to you!

Many good carpeting plants can be found in the 'alpine' section of garden centres and nursery catalogues. These are generally dense or creeping in habit, and although they may look minute on purchase, some are capable of covering quite a lot of ground in a fairly short time. Acaena, ajugas and saxifrages can all be used to advantage as ground cover with very little after-care once established.

Once you have taken all these basic considerations into account, the final choice will largely rely upon personal preferences. While most people would, given the choice, probably opt for low-growing

INTRODUCTION

evergreens, the use of some deciduous shrubs prevents the repetitive look which sometimes appears with mass plantings of things which do not alter their appearance much throughout the year. However, if you are a keen observer, you will notice that, even with these, the new spring foliage is usually a different colour, while many take on a red or pinkish tinge in winter, and there could be flowers or berries to increase the interest.

Furthermore, with deciduous plants, you get the opportunity to introduce a different kind of concept by underplanting with spring, or even hardy summer, bulbs if the ground cover is not too tall. Larger bulbs – daffodils and narcissi are excellent in this respect – are used among taller shrubs, and shorter ones (like crocuses) with ground-hugging plants. It is surprising to see just how dense a planting bulbs will manage to fight their way through, providing the whole area is adequately and regularly fed and watered.

Herbaceous perennials, especially those that die back to leave bare earth in winter, are not everyone's cup of tea, although you can get very good results with many, particularly those which retain their leaves in winter, like hellebores, some euphorbias and some hardy geraniums. Plants that do disappear completely provide an ideal opportunity to have a really good clean-up, for example where the area is affected by large numbers of falling leaves, which are often extremely difficult to remove when they become trapped in the branches of shrubs.

Against this could be set the argument that many herbaceous perennials used in ground-cover schemes, in particular hostas and hermerocallis (day lilies) produce flowers on long stalks which look untidy once the flowering season is over, and are better removed, thus adding to the work-load. The same argument applies to some roses which are recommended for ground cover; they can look scruffy if not dead-headed. The answer to this is to choose species which form hips after flowering, like that rugosa shrub 'Frau Dagmar Hastrup' which has long been a favourite for mass planting.

Many wall shrubs will make really good ground cover. The best of these are those of lax growth which are generally grown up a wall to support them, like *Cotoneaster horizontalis, Pyracantha* 'Soleil d'Or' and chaenomeles, the Japanese quince. This idea can be taken a step further by using true climbing plants, like wistaria, clematis and Virginia creeper. Many such plants will ramble away quite happily, again often rooting where they touch the soil, though some pegging down may be necessary in the early stages. Rambler roses can also be used in the same way. This form of ground cover is not so much practical as interesting. It is fine if you want a look that is really different, but it is not the least labour-intensive way to cover a patch of earth.

If you use a great deal of the normal sort of low-growing ground cover, you may find that your garden looks rather flat, unless you have obvious dips and rises. This is where introducing taller shrubs will pay dividends. Generally speaking, this kind of subject should be positioned towards the back and away from the property, though block plantings of taller species can be used to hide or divide some of the garden, introducing an element of surprise.

A final point that you will always have to consider is whether the bed is in full sun, partial shade, or even full shade. A ground-cover scheme can be equally effective in any of these locations provided that what is used is chosen with care. The essence of this type of planting is that everything must always be in the rudest of health, not only to do the job properly but for appearance's sake. Nobody wants a large piece of garden occupied by sickly plants which are struggling to survive.

Estimating the number of plants needed

When we normally think of planting something in the garden, it is likely to be seen as an individual plant, and therefore the distance between the specimens is quite important. Put too close together, one will crowd another out, the stronger-growing of them smothering the weaker. With a ground-cover scheme, however, whole pieces of land are covered with either the same variety of plant, or ones of similar habit, and it is the overall result which matters, not the individual specimen. For this reason, and because complete coverage is required as quickly as possible, it is not necessary to space plants as far apart as they would be if they were only used in single numbers; in fact, it is desirable to close up the distances quite a lot in order to get things moving.

It is not really possible to give a firm rule for every plant likely to be used in such a planting, but as a very rough guide, strong-growing low shrubs can be planted about 2 feet (60 cm) apart, less strong-growing ones roughly 18 inches (45 cm) apart, and

INTRODUCTION

cushion-forming species like heathers and saxifrages 9–12 inches (22–30 cm) apart. In the case of taller shrubs I find that to position them about twice as close as they would be if used as individual specimens is a guide, though if you are prepared to wait longer for the full effect, the normal spacing or just closing up slightly on this is quite adequate, especially where more expensive varieties are chosen. With herbaceous ground cover, it is usually all right to stick to the recommended spacing for the individual plant, or, if you are in a hurry, closing up a little. However, once you know what species you are going to use, and have checked on what they do and how quickly they do it, you can work out spacings much more accurately.

Having decided how far apart the plants should be positioned, the next thing is to find out how many you are going to need. If you want to be really fussy, you can draw the bed or area out to scale on graph paper and mark in every plant at the correct spacing. There is, however, a much easier way than this.

Work out the area of ground you are planting up – if it is an awkward shape, the best way to do this is to divide it on paper into a series of rectangles and triangles – then take the planting distance and square it, and finally divide the second sum into the first. The answer will give you enough plants to fill the bed; the exact positions can be decided upon and adjusted when you come to planting up. For example, imagine you have a piece of ground which can be divided up into a rectangle 30 feet × 20 feet (9 m × 6 m) and a right-angled triangle 30 feet × 10 feet (9 m × 3 m). The area is 30 feet × 20 feet (9 m × 6 m) = 600 sq. feet (54 m^2) plus ½ × 30 feet × 10 feet (9 m × 3 m) = 150 sq. feet (13.5 m^2), which is 750 sq. feet (nearly 70 m^2). If your plants are to be placed 18 inches (45 cm) apart, you will need 750 sq. feet ÷ (1½ feet × 1½ feet) [70 m^2 ÷ (0.45 × 0.45)]. You will generally find that if you order in tens, twenties or whatever, nurseries will give you a discount, so you may be better off financially if you round the quantity up or down. Bearing this in mind, the number you require is 350! Quite a lot, isn't it?

17

Ground cover for large, open areas

The vast majority of sites which are potential candidates for ground-cover schemes are in an open position, and are therefore not affected by the shade from trees or buildings. These are the sort of areas you want to look attractive with the least ultimate effort. They lend themselves to mass planting with low-growing and medium-sized shrubs which do not need specialist cultivation, prostrate and spreading conifers, and a variety of herbaceous plants with either good, dense foliage or the attribute of spreading rapidly but not untidily. The main object – apart from smothering weeds and filling the space efficiently – is to be visually effective, and so the subjects must look good, generally both individually and massed together. (Many of the following suggested species will also do well in situations other than open and sunny.)

Low-growing and medium-sized evergreen shrubs
Berberis candidula and *B. candidula* **'Amstelveen'** are useful in positions likely to be tempting to vandals. They have an arching habit and reach about 2½ feet (80 cm) in height, with small, dark green leaves bluish-white on the undersides; purple berries appear in the autumn. Normally no pruning is necessary. The plants should be spaced about 2 feet (60 cm) apart initially.

Berberis media **'Parkjeweel'** also reaches about 2½ feet (80 cm), again with a slightly arching habit. It is very prickly, with quite large leaves (which turn red in the autumn), and plenty of golden yellow flowers in early summer. Again no pruning is necessary, but if the plants tend to get out of hand they can be trimmed with a pair of shears or hedgetrimmer (and full riot gear!). Space the plants about 2 feet (60 cm) apart.

Berberis verruculosa is another arching shrub, which also spreads by slightly underground suckering stems. The flowers are yellow, followed by black berries. The leaves on older plants are tinted red. Space the plants about 2 feet (60 cm) apart.

Note: most berberis will tolerate some shade providing it is not too dense.

Ceanothus thyrsiflorus 'Repens' (creeping blue blossom). One of the hardiest ceanothus, this has a semi-prostrate habit and quickly forms a spreading mound up to about 3 feet (1 m) in height. It produces a mass of mid-blue flowers in May and needs no pruning. Initial spacing is 3–4 feet (1–1.3 m) apart.

Cornus canadensis (creeping dogwood) is not particularly happy in alkaline soil, but I have included it here as in a neutral to acid soil it colonizes large areas rapidly, spreading by suckers. The plants only grow about 6 inches (15 cm) high, and mass plantings look quite spectacular in autumn when the leaves turn wine-red. It has white bracts in summer followed by red berries. Initial spacing should be 12–15 inches (30–38 cm). *C. canadensis* is not keen on dry, sandy soils; some moisture should be present at all times for best results. It will tolerate light shade as well as open locations. If the plants begin to look straggly they can be clipped over in spring.

Cotoneaster humifusus (dammeri) and **'Skogholm Coral Beauty'** are two quite prostrate, evergreen forms of this genus which root into the soil where they touch. They produce red or orange berries and need no pruning. A wide range of conditions is tolerated quite good-naturedly. Space the plants 2 feet (60 cm) apart.

Cornus canadensis

THE BIG COVER-UP

Cotoneaster congestus is a less rampant carpeting shrub for smaller areas. As it is slower-growing the plants need to be spaced initially at about 12 inches (30 cm) to ensure coverage in a reasonable time.

Cotoneaster conspicuus **'Decorus'**, **C. horizontalis** and **C. microphyllus** have arching branches and will form hummocks if not planted against a fence or wall. *C. horizontalis*, the fishbone cotoneaster, is deciduous, but sheds its leaves late in the season, after they have turned a magnificent bright red, and tends to come into leaf very early the next season. As it is covered with red berries for most of the winter (birds permitting), there is hardly a day when it looks uninteresting. The variegated form is much less strong-growing, but in the right position an established planting has an almost 'frosty' effect. *C. conspicuus* has particularly pretty white flowers in early summer. *C. microphyllus* produces very large red berries. As their flowers are attractive to bees and birds love the berries, these cotoneasters are good for bringing wildlife into the garden. Initial spacings are 2½–3 feet (80 cm–1 m).

Many forms of **heather**, such as *Erica cinerea* (bell heather), *E. tetralix* (cross-leaved heath), and *E. vulgaris* (now known as Calluna) the Scottish heather or ling will only thrive in an acid soil. However, there are certain species, such as *Erica carnea* (usually referred to as winter-flowering heather), *E.* × *darleyensis*, *E. erigena* and *E. vagans* (Cornish heath) which will tolerate some lime in the soil providing it is not too alkaline.

The lowest-growing heathers are varieties of *Erica carnea*, such as the golden-leaved 'Anne Sparkes' and 'Foxhollow', the dark-foliaged, red-flowered 'Myretoun Ruby' and 'Vivellii', and the strong-growing 'Springwood White'. *Erica darleyensis* grows to about 1½ feet (45 cm) and usually has pink or white flowers according to cultivar. The Cornish heath flowers in late summer, again with pink or white flowers, but the dead flower heads are attractive so should be allowed to remain on the bushes throughout the winter. They can be removed in the spring when the bushes are trimmed. (It is good practice to clip all heathers over after flowering as otherwise they tend to get woody at the base.) *Erica erigena* is a taller-growing lime-tolerant heather, some varieties, such as 'Brightness' can reach 3 feet (1 m). Bear this in mind when working out the positions of various forms of heather, placing the taller species where they do not hide the shorter ones.

A mass planting of heathers is one of the most effective methods of

GROUND COVER FOR LARGE, OPEN AREAS

ground cover there is, and if spaced in the first instance fairly close together (about 12 inches – 30 cm), they soon run into each other to form a weed-proof barrier. If heathers are planted slightly deeper than they were in the container, the buried stems will also root, making the ground cover more efficient. An annual top-dressing of peat will also encourage stem-rooting and help to prevent the woody appearance often encountered in mature beds.

A few years ago, heather gardens (often including conifers) were all the rage; more recently they have become less popular because they tend to look too much the same whatever the time of year. While I would tend to agree, they still have a lot going for them, especially with modern architecture, and if it comes to a choice between a rubbish dump and a heather garden, there is really no contest. Furthermore, if the right species are chosen, and a reasonable amount of maintenance given regularly, then they can look very good.

There are many plain green and variegated cultivars of **Euonymus fortunei** which are first rate for ground cover, as the evergreen leaves are dense and many forms will produce roots along the stems, especially if they should happen to become covered with soil or mulch. The most well-known variety, 'Silver Queen', used to be known as *Euonymus radicans* 'Variegata', and will also climb if planted against a vertical surface. Other variegated ones are 'Emerald Gaiety', 'Emerald 'n Gold', 'Golden Prince', 'Gold Tip', 'Sheridan Gold', and 'Sunspot', whose names are fairly descriptive, I think. Block plantings of several variegated cultivars are effective, or the brighter colour can be broken up with all-green groups like 'Colorata', 'Dart's Blanket', 'Emerald Cushion' or 'Vegatus', which often develop purple tints in autumn and winter. The plants can be improved in appearance by trimming them over with a hedge trimmer or shears in spring. Initial spacing of the plants should be 1½–2 feet (45–60 cm) apart. They can be planted in shade if not too dense.

Genistas are closely related to Cytisus, the true brooms, but in general make better ground cover, both regarding their spreading habit and their tendency to live longer. *Genista hispanica,* the Spanish gorse, makes a low-growing, spiny hummock, with golden flowers in early summer. Another hummock-forming shrub is *Genista lydia,* which produces green, wiry stems and has profuse yellow flowers, again in early summer. *Genista pilosa* has a carpeting habit, reaching no more than about 6 inches (15 cm) in height, with yellow racemes of flowers in May. *Genista tinctoria* 'Royal Gold' is a more upright grower, with green stems reaching about 2 feet (60 cm).

Genistas do have small deciduous leaves, but their out-of-flower effect is created by their bright green shoots, and as the colour is maintained throughout the winter, I have classed them here as evergreens. They can become somewhat straggly in time, so it is useful to remove some of the newer growths immediately after flowering, but make sure you do not cut back into the old wood, as the plants will often not regrow from this. Spacing should be about 1½ feet (45 cm), but this can be closed up a bit for quick effect.

The low-growing members of the **hebe** family are excellent for ground cover and are much more hardy than their taller, larger-leaved counterparts. *Hebe albicans* has greyish-green, oblong leaves and white flowers, and grows to about 1½ feet (45 cm). Initial spacing is 1½–2 feet (45–60 cm). *H. anomala* makes a rounded bush about 3 feet (1 m) across, with bright, yellowish-green, small leaves and white, starry flowers in the second half of summer. Spacing should be 2–2½ feet (60–80 cm) apart.

H. armstrongii is one of my favourites. It has unusual 'whipcord'-like branches, almost reminiscent of a conifer, and warm yellow foliage, with small white flowers in summer. It should be spaced about 15 inches (38 cm) apart for good results as a ground cover plant. Other 'whipcord' hebes which can be used in the same way are the grey-green *H. cupressoides* and one with a similar colouring to *H. armstrongii*, *H. ocracea* 'James Stirling', which is smaller and has a more spreading yet compact habit. Successful spacing for this plant is 12 inches (30 cm).

H. brachysyphon and *H. buxifolia* are similar in leaf form to *H. anomala*, but they are darker. *H. brachysyphon* is the larger of the two, reaching about 4½ feet (1.5 m) in time, while *H. buxifolia* rarely gets more than 2 feet (80 cm). Spacing is about 2½ feet (80 cm) for *H. brachysyphon;* 15–18 inches (38–45 cm) for *H. buxifolia*.

H. 'Carl Teschner' is an ideal ground-cover plant. It has low-growing, arching branches with very small, box-like leaves on stems which are almost black when young. The flowers are exceptionally pretty, violet with a white throat in small racemes during midsummer. It roots where it touches and so can colonize an area of ground quite quickly.

H. pimeloides 'Quicksilver' is semi-prostrate, again with blackish stems, bearing silvery-blue leaves and white flowers in May. It also roots where it touches. Space the plants 15 inches (38 cm) apart. Another hebe with grey leaves and a like habit is *H. pinguifolia* 'Pagei'. Like 'Quicksilver' it reaches about 12 inches (30 cm) in height and roots along the stems where they are in contact with the soil. The flowers are white, with the main flush in June and a few produced again later in the summer.

H. 'Wingletye' has flowers which resemble those of *H.* 'Carl Teschner' and foliage not unlike 'Pagei', though it is more prostrate than either, reaching only about 4 inches (10 cm) in height. Spacing should be 12 inches (30 cm) or closer, as it is quite slow-growing.

You may find that, after some years, many hebes tend to become straggly and woody at the base, at which stage they can be cut hard

Hebe 'Wingletye'

back as they will quickly form a mass of new shoots from low down. To avoid any frost damage, it is advisable to do this in the spring. You may lose some flowers the first season after pruning, but the end results justify the action. Alternatively, most hebes respond well to a light clipping with shears every year, preferably after flowering.

Lonicera nitida 'Baggesen's Gold'. It seems hardly possible that this attractive shrub is the golden relative of that hateful hedging plant, Lonicera nitida, which usually looks like a badly constructed bird's nest, needs cutting every half-hour (well, almost) and will promptly root from any stray scrap of the clippings to become almost as invasive as the most pernicious weed if not dealt with promptly. L. n. 'Baggesen's Gold' also needs clipping to maintain a good shape and an optimum height of about 4 feet (1.2 m), but it is a delightful gold colour, even in light shade, the best colour being obtained on the new shoots. It is unexacting, can be raided regularly and without detriment by the flower arranger, and will recover quickly if damaged, so making useful cover where vandal activity is likely. Spacing is about 3 feet (1 m) apart.

Stranvaesia davidiana 'Prostrata' is related to cotoneaster, but the leaves look slightly different, although the bushes have white flowers and red berries in a similar way. The prostrate form of stranvaesia is quite slow, so should be spaced about 18 inches (45 cm) apart, or closer if the budget will allow. S. davidiana 'Prostrata' will tolerate some shade, but can be damaged by frost in hard winters, so should not be positioned in too inclement a spot.

Low-growing deciduous shrubs

As you will have gathered from comments in the first chapter, these do not have the same advantages as evergreens where ground cover is concerned, but there are a few shrubs which are capable of making enough of a splash in summer, and are also dense enough to suppress weeds, to merit consideration. However, because masses of bare twigs can look fairly monotonous in winter, it is advisable to include blocks of evergreens in any scheme using deciduous shrubs as ground-cover subjects. These will tend to take the eye off the bare stems until they start to stir again in spring.

Berberis thunbergii 'Atropopurea Nana' reaches about 2 feet (60 cm) in height and has striking purple leaves, yellow flowers in early summer, red fruit in autumn, and colours up well before losing its leaves, so it can look quite spectacular when massed. It is also excellent for high-risk areas likely to be under siege from vandals. Initial spacing is 18 inches (45 cm). Regular pruning is unnecessary, but the bushes can be clipped if required.

Berberis thunbergii 'Green Carpet' grows about 4½ feet (1.5 m) across, and less than 3 feet (1 m) high. The light green leaves turn brilliantly in autumn and it produces a good quantity of red berries. This is another usefully prickly plant, but like all members of the berberis family, mass plantings can be murder to look after in their formative years and stout clothing is strongly advised. Spacing 2½–3 feet (80 cm–1 m).

'Harlequin' is another thunbergii cultivar, which grows to about 4½ feet (1.5 m) and has speckled white, pinkish-purple leaves. Spacing is 3 feet (1 m) apart. 'Rose Glow' is rather the same, with purple leaves mottled pink and silver, but this variegation fades with maturity. A smaller form of thunbergii is 'Kobold' which has glossy, dark green leaves with grey undersides. Spacing for this is about 15 inches (38 cm).

Berberis wilsonae is suitable as a ground-cover shrub because of its shapely but spreading habit. At maturity it is about 3 feet (1 m) tall and almost evergreen. The leaves turn red and orange in autumn and blend well with the coral red berries. Initial spacing should be 2 feet (60 cm) apart.

Chaenomeles speciosa 'Simonii'. Many of the ornamental quinces will make good ground-cover plants if planted in open ground, but this one is particularly effective as it has a naturally low-growing habit. It has semi-double, very dark red flowers in spring and in some seasons will produce edible fruit. There is some shade tolerance, but the best flowers are produced in a sunny spot. Pruning is not normally necessary, but if you need to keep the plants within bounds they should be shortened back immediately after flowering. Space the plants 3 feet (1 m) apart.

Hypericum forrestii produces saucer-shaped, golden yellow flowers and bronzy seed pods on well-shaped bushes with erect main stems having horizontal side branches. It grows to about 3 feet (1 m) and can be left unpruned or cut hard back periodically according to the type of area being covered. *H. elatum* 'Elstead' also has bronzy-orange seed pods but the flowers are smaller, although borne in large numbers. These two shrubs should be spaced 2 feet (60 cm) apart – a little more if you are economizing. *H. patulum* 'Hidcote' is semi-evergreen (except in hard winters) and makes a larger bush than *H. forestii* and *H. elatum* 'Elstead', reaching about 4½ feet (1.5 m) if left unpruned. It is rarely without flower during summer, the golden, saucer-shaped blooms sometimes as much as 3 inches (7 cm) across. Initial spacing should be 3 feet (1 m) apart.

The **potentilla** genus includes some of the finest small and medium shrubs available. They nearly all flower throughout the summer, so choice is mainly one of personal taste in flower colour and suitable size, but those potentillas with a naturally spreading habit, and especially those which do not grow too tall (they look rather messy when the leaves are off and need to be as inconspicuous as possible during winter) are the most appropriate to ground-cover plantings. Potentillas will grow and flower in light shade, but in heavier shade they will become straggly and the flowering potential will be seriously reduced. No regular pruning is necessary, but a light clipping of the mature bushes will help to keep them looking neat. Spacing is usually about 2 feet (60 cm) apart.

The following are some of the most recommended potentillas for mass planting. 'Abbotswood', with white flowers and grey foliage; 2½ feet (80 cm) tall. 'Elizabeth', with primrose flowers from midsummer onwards. 'Longacre' has a spreading habit, the bushes no more than 2 feet (60 cm) tall when fully grown. The flowers are very large and pale yellow. *Potentilla mandschurica* is another spreader, only growing about 12 inches (30 cm) tall. It has white flowers and grey foliage. Yet another with a spreading habit, 'Primrose Beauty' is taller, attaining 3 feet (1 m) in good conditions. This potentilla has primrose-yellow flowers and grey-green leaves. 'Red Ace' has unusual-coloured flowers for a shrubby potentilla: bright orange-red with yellow undersides to the petals. It also spreads and forms a bush wider than it is high, not growing more than 18 inches (45 cm) tall after several years. It will fade in very strong sunshine but otherwise is an attractive and different low-maintenance plant. Another curiously coloured potentilla, 'Royal Flush', is rose-pink with a yellow centre, and sometimes semi-double. The habit is similar to 'Red Ace', although the bush itself is smaller. It also fades in hot sunshine until it can become almost white. 'Sunset', an older cultivar with reddish flowers, is wider-spreading than most, sometimes reaching more than 4 feet (1.2 m) in diameter. 'Tangerine' is semi-prostrate, with flower

GROUND COVER FOR LARGE, OPEN AREAS

Potentilla 'Longacre'

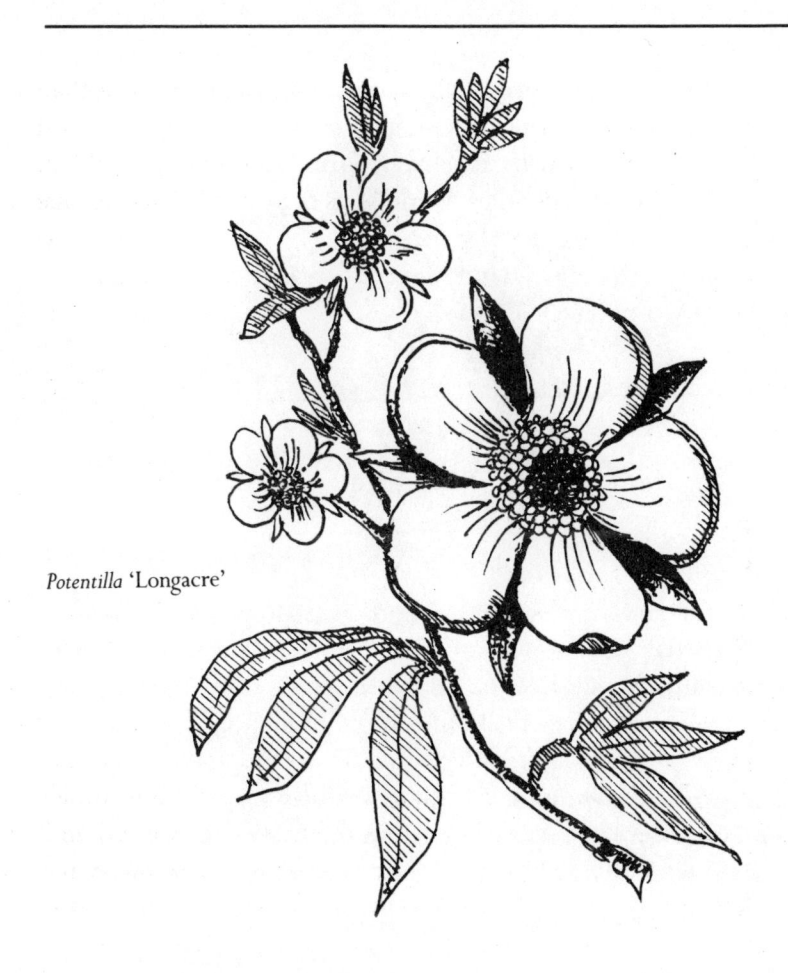

colour ranging from copper-red in light shade and cool conditions to yellow in really sunny places. Height 12–18 inches (30–45 cm). 'Tilford Cream' grows about as tall as 'Tangerine' but does not spread as far. It has large, creamy white flowers.

There are several **dwarf willows** which could be used as ground cover, but perhaps the most fitting of all is *Salix lanata*, the woolly willow, with silvery-grey, fleecy leaves and grey and yellow 'pussy' catkins in spring. It makes a bush about 3 feet by 4 feet (1m by 1.2 m) and needs to be spaced about 2½ feet (80 cm) apart for good coverage. Another willow, with a prostrate habit which does well on sandy soil and in maritime areas, is *S. repens argentea,* which also has yellow catkins and silvery leaves. Spacing is the same as for *S. lanata*.

There are several small **shrubby spiraeas** which can be massed

THE BIG COVER-UP

Salix lanata

to give good cover to an open piece of ground. Most of these benefit from hard annual pruning in spring, which improves the leaf coverage, encourages good colour in those which have leaves other than green, and prevents the bushes from becoming too woody at the base.

Spiraea nipponica 'Snowmound' is a dense shrub up to about 3 feet (1 m) high and covered in small white flowers in June. Initial spacing is 2–2½ feet (60–80 cm). *Spiraea thunbergii* reaches about the same height as 'Snowmound', but has a more spreading habit. The white flowers are produced very early in the season – usually from February to April. Space plants 2½ feet (80 cm) apart.

Spiraea × *bumalda* 'Anthony Waterer' is a well-known, twiggy shrub with green leaves which are sometimes variegated cream and pink. It grows to about 2½ feet (80 cm) in height by as much across, and bears flat, fluffy heads of carmine-red flowers recurrently from July to September. A plant not dissimilar in appearance, though without the variegations, is *Spiraea japonica* 'Shirobana' which is unusual in that the flower heads can be white and rosy-red on the same plant, and indeed on the same branch or twig. Spacing is the same for both shrubs, 2–2½ feet (60–80 cm), depending on the speed at which you want the ground covered. 'Goldflame' resembles 'Anthony Waterer' in shape, but the leaves are yellow, and unfold bright red in spring. On certain plants there can be odd leaves distinctly variegated gold and green. It is a most desirable shrub, even

Spiraea 'Anthony Waterer'

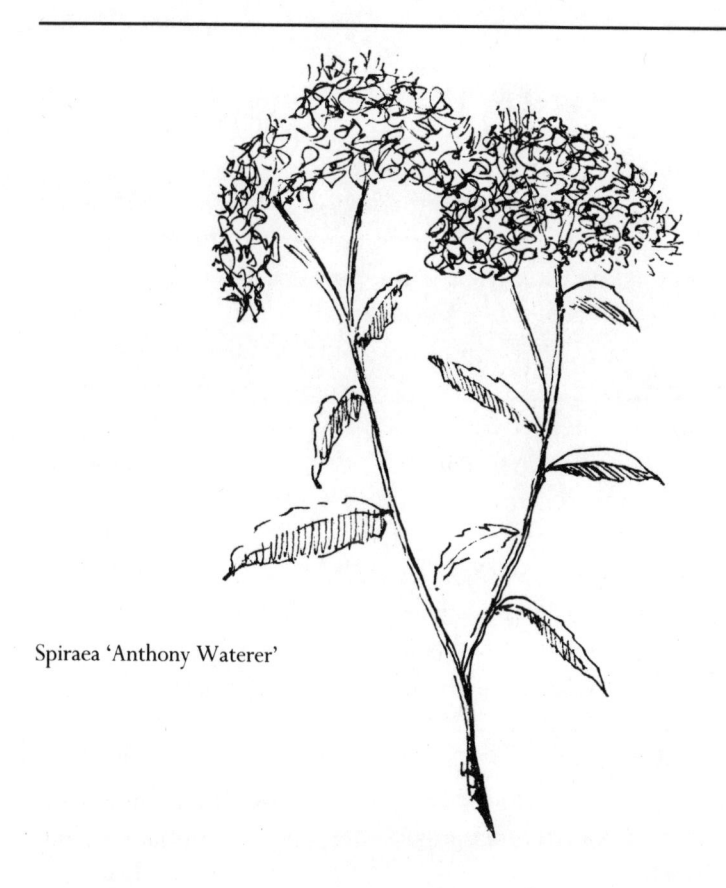

as a single specimen; massed together they can be quite astounding, especially early in the season. 'Goldmound' is also yellow, though not as deep in colour, and the young leaves are not as bright. It is a much smaller bush, growing not more than about 2 feet (60 cm) high, and has pink flowers.

Spiraea japonica 'Alpina' is a cushion-forming dwarf shrub which makes excellent ground cover for the front of a scheme. It is about 15 inches (38 cm) tall with flat pink flower heads in late spring and early summer and green leaves which colour well in autumn. 'Little Princess' is a slightly larger version. Spacings for 'Goldmound' and 'Little Princess', and the golden form of the latter, 'Golden Princess', are about 18 inches (45 cm); for 'Alpina' the plants would need to be positioned about 12 inches (30 cm) apart.

Stephanandra incisa 'Crispa' is a mound-forming shrub, with small, crinkly leaves, arching stems with noticeable brown bark and tiny, cream flowers in June.

Conifers

Spreading conifers, especially junipers, have been used for many years as ground cover, but in modern gardens they should be chosen with care, as there are a few which are temptingly good-looking as young plants, but develop into monsters, although if you have a very large area to fill they can be useful as you will not need to plant so many! Prostrate and spreading junipers are also handy in that, unlike most other conifers, they will survive some shade and dryness at the roots, though it is not a particularly good idea to plant them in positions where they could be under stress when there are so many other things that would be much happier with such conditions.

Junipers are not the only conifers with prostrate and semi-prostrate varieties. All conifers, even the upright forms, are first-rate for ground cover as the dense, evergreen, resinous foliage soon daunts even the most adventurous weed. Where conditions are right – open, well-drained but not too dry – there is an enormous selection to choose from; the main limitations being the size of the area and the amount of money you wish to lay out, which can be quite considerable where some of the smaller, slower, but nonetheless ideal modern garden conifers are concerned. However, if the space you want to cover is not large, you may find that about three of certain subjects would be adequate, so the cost may not be prohibitive after all.

The following is a list of some of the most efficient ground cover conifers available today, and the size of area for which they are most suited.

Cedrus deodara **'Golden Horizon'** is quite a slow-growing form of cedar and as the plants have usually been grafted they can be quite expensive, but it is such a lovely thing, with golden-needled cascading branches, that it could be worth planting a group of three in a prime position. Space about 2½ feet (80 cm) for best effect.

Chamaecyparis pisifera **'Filifera Aurea'** makes unusual ground cover. It has a spreading, mop-headed habit, with golden, thread-like foliage, and will eventually reach about 3 feet (1 m) across, so for quick establishment the plants need to be positioned about 2 feet (60 cm) apart.

Juniperus communis **'Depressa Aurea'** is a prostrate or semi-prostrate conifer with golden foliage which turns bronze in autumn. It grows to about 12 inches (30 cm) in height, and will

GROUND COVER FOR LARGE, OPEN AREAS

eventually spread to about 4½ feet (1.5 m). Space plants about 3 feet (1 m) apart. There are many other forms of *J. communis* which make good ground-cover subjects. 'Hornbrookii' is at first completely prostrate, but eventually builds up in the centre to give some height. It spreads to about 6 feet (2 m) in time. The foliage turns bronze as the year progresses. Plants should be spaced 3 feet (1 m) apart. 'Green Carpet' is a slower form, growing very close to the ground, with bright green foliage in summer. Ultimately it will spread to about 3 feet (1 m) so ideal spacing is 1½–2 feet (45–60 cm). 'Repanda' has been widely available for many years. It is quite vigorous, soon covering about 4½ feet (1.5 m). Space plants about 2–2½ feet (60–80 cm).

Juniperus davurica **'Expansa Aureospicata'** is a striking spreading conifer with green foliage flecked with bright yellow. Eventually, it will cover about 4 feet (1.2 m), so space plants about 2 feet (60 cm) apart.

Juniperus horizontalis has produced many excellent low-growing cultivars with both green and greyish foliage, which generally have a feathery appearance. 'Banff' is silvery-blue and spreads about 3 feet (1 m). Spacing should be 2 feet (60 cm). 'Blue Chip' is somewhat alike, but the foliage turns blue-grey in winter. It will spread about 4½ feet (1.5 m) and should be spaced 2½ feet (80 cm) apart, though this spacing can be closed up for quicker coverage. 'Glauca' grows quite flat, with steely-blue foliage. 'Wiltonii' is a slower version. 'Emerald Spreader' is also quite flat, with pleasant, emerald-green foliage. Spacing for these three is the same as for 'Blue Chip'. 'Turquoise Spreader' is rather the same, though slower, and not so wide-reaching, with turquoise-green foliage. Space plants 2 feet (60 cm) apart. 'Hughes' is not prostrate, but the branches are wide and ascending, and a pleasant silver in colour. It can cover more than 6 feet (2m) in time, so is unsuitable for small areas. Space plants about 2½–3 feet (80 cm–1 m) apart. 'Plumosa Youngstown' is semi-prostrate, grey-green in summer and bronze-tinted in winter. It spreads up to 3 feet (1m), so the spacing should be 2 feet (60 cm). 'Prince of Wales' spreads about the same distance but is much flatter. The foliage is bright green in summer, and flecked with brownish-purple in winter. Spacing is the same as for 'Plumosa Youngstown'.

Juniperus × *media* is a large group of conifers which includes some admirable ground-cover subjects for small gardens and some real giants as far as spreading conifers are concerned. It is essential to know the habit of the type you are looking at before making a mistake. 'Blue and Gold' is a delightful, moderate-growing form, with blue-grey foliage splashed with yellow. It will grow to about 3 feet (1m) in height and spread about 4½ feet (1.5 m). Space plants about 2½–3 feet (80 cm–1 m) apart.

'Gold Coast' and 'Old Gold' are more restrained versions of the once over-planted 'Pfitzeriana' and 'Pfitzeriana Aurea', so often seen as horrible mistakes on rockeries. These two do have their uses where space is available, and admittedly planted in groups they are quite something, but even one needs a lot of room, although in an emergency they will stand cutting back more than some conifers will. 'Gold Coast' is slightly more compact than 'Old Gold' and keeps its colour better in winter. 'Old Gold' can grow to as much as 4½ feet (1.5 m) across and up to 3 feet (1 m) – occasionally more – in height. Spacing for 'Pfitzeriana' and 'Pfitzeriana Aurea' is 4 feet (1.2 m) or more. For 'Gold Coast' spacing is 2–2½ feet (60–80 cm) apart, and for 'Old Gold' 2½–3 feet (80 cm–1 m). 'Gold Sovereign' is a very slow-growing sport of 'Old Gold'; it is much flatter and the colour is better. A small group is ideal as ground cover in a modern garden, and should be spaced 2 feet (60 cm) apart.

'Sulphur Spray' is semi-prostrate, with a whitish tinge to the foliage, especially in summer. It will spread to about 4½ feet (1.5 m) and should be spaced about 2½ feet (80 cm) apart. 'Procumbens Nana' has a completely prostrate habit, and cheery apple-green foliage. It has quite a wide coverage after a few years. Space plants 2½–3 feet (80 cm–1 m) apart.

Juniperus sabina 'Tamariscifolia' is another widely planted conifer, with a flat growth habit, but the branches build up layer upon layer until it reaches about 18 inches (45 cm) in height, with a spread of about 4½ feet (1.5 m). 'Variegata' is smaller, spreading less than 3 feet (1 m). Spacing for 'Tamariscifolia' is 2½–3 feet (80 cm–1 m) and for 'Variegata' 2–2½ feet (60–80 cm).

Juniperus squamata is a group which contains some very good ground-cover plants. 'Blue Carpet' is a strong-growing, not quite prostrate conifer, which can cover well over 6 feet (2 m) and has bright, silvery-blue foliage. Space plants about 3–4 feet (1–1.2 m).

Closely planted shrubs, including *Cornus siberica* 'Spaethii'

Weeds cannot penetrate this close planting of *Cotinus* 'Royal Purple', *Weigela florida* 'Variegata', *Prunus cistena*, variegated ground elder and *Dicentra* 'Adrian Bloom'

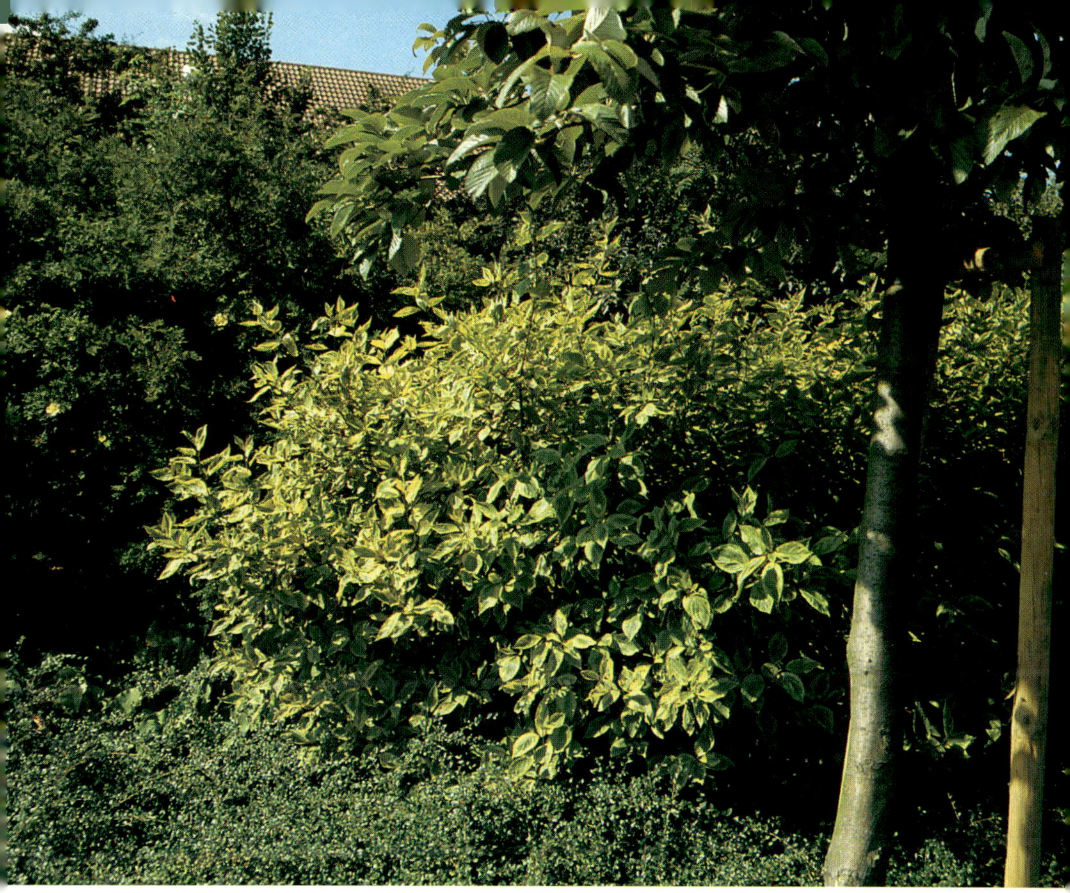

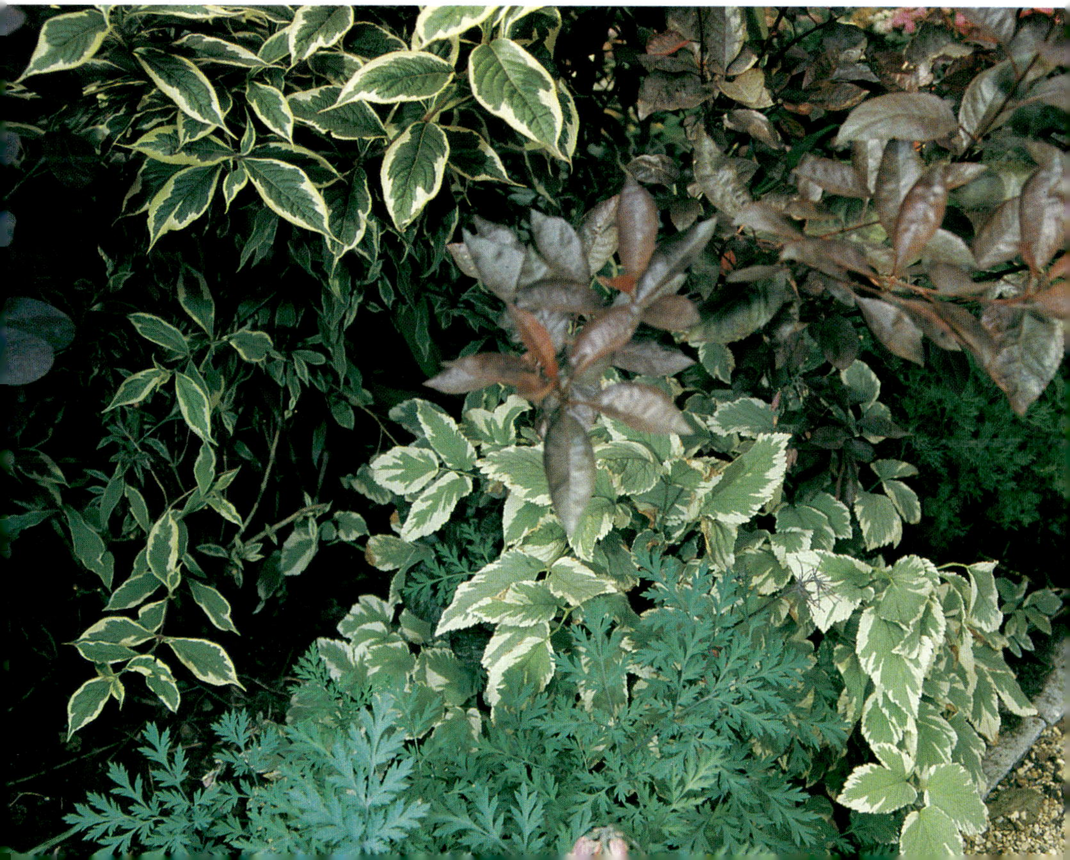

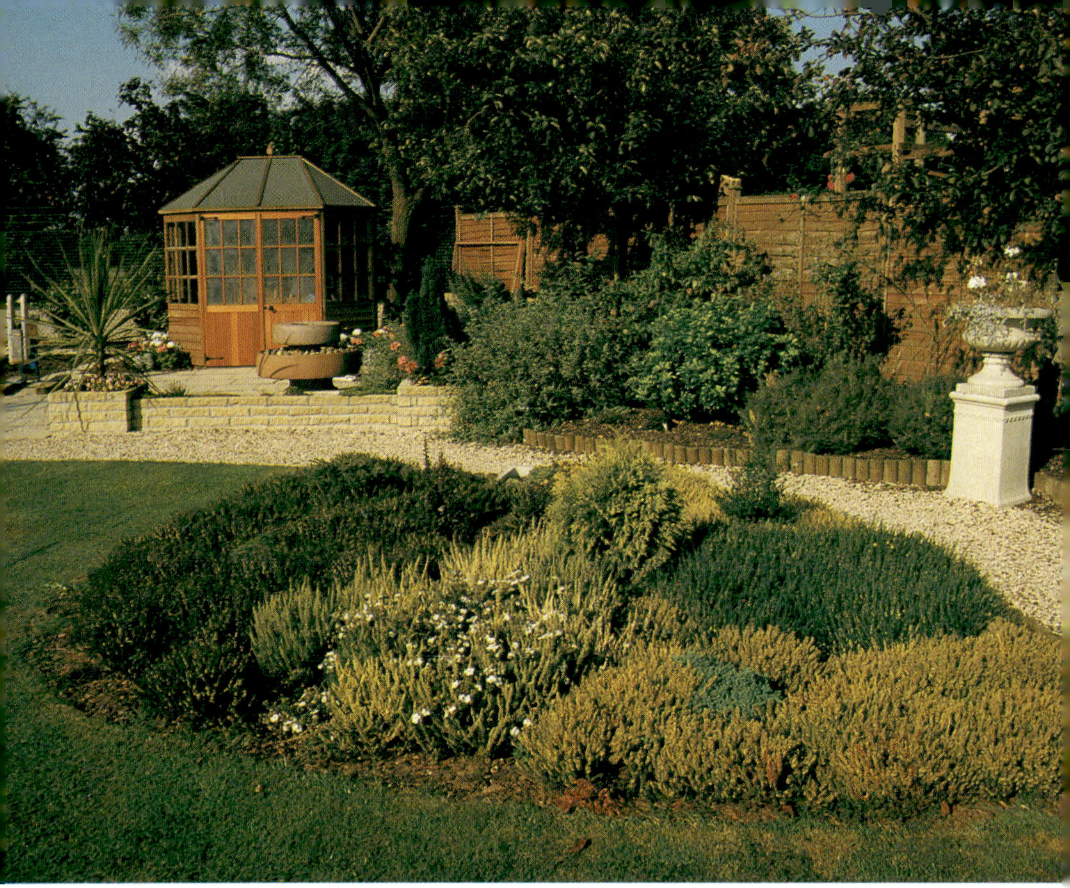

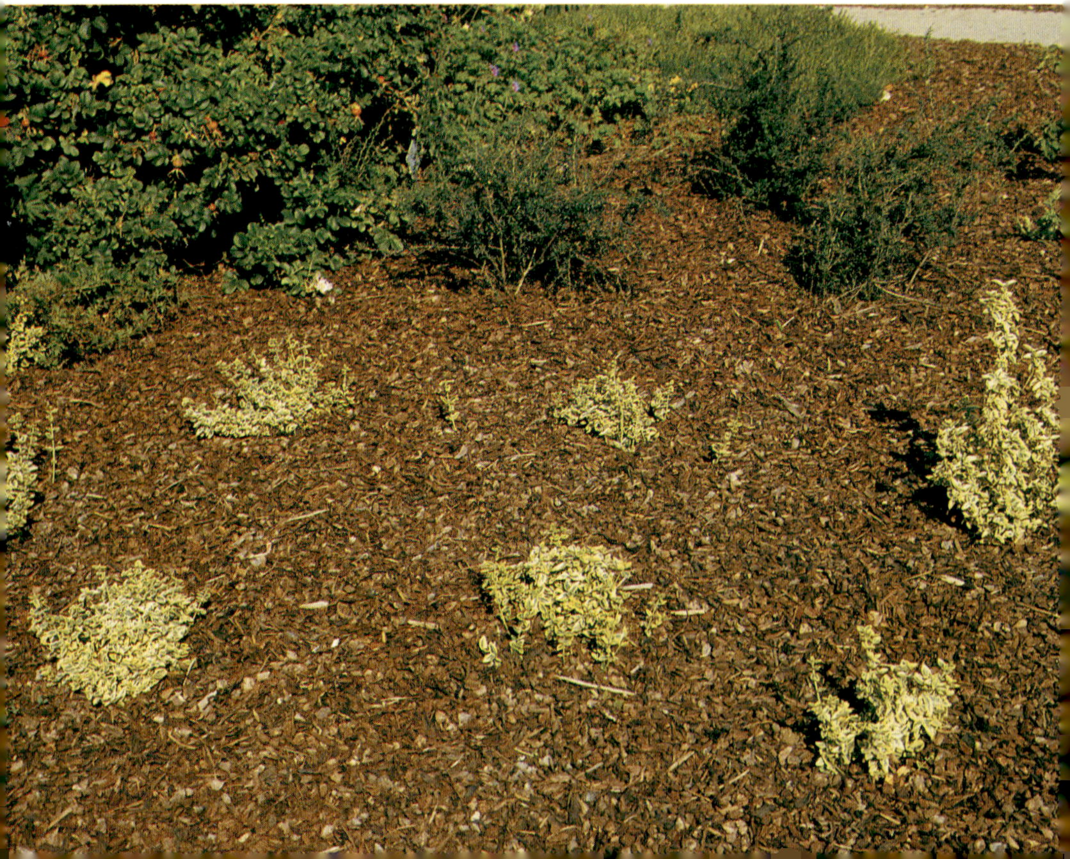

'Blue Star' is a much smaller, less spreading form which can be mass-planted to cover a moderate-sized piece of ground eventually, but it will take time. It should be spaced at 1½–2-foot (45–60-cm) intervals in order to get some effect without too long a wait.

Juniperus taxifolia lutchuensis has deep green foliage and a prostrate yet compact habit. It will eventually grow to about 4 feet (1.2 m) across. Space plants 2–2½ feet (60–80 cm) apart for best effect.

Juniperus virginiana 'Grey Owl' is a very strong-growing, semi-prostrate conifer with light grey foliage and a coverage of about 6 feet (2 m). Spacing is 3 feet (1m) between plants.

Microbiota decussata, a low-growing conifer with dense, lacy foliage turning bronze in winter, has a spread of about 4½ feet (1.5 m). Space plants about 2½–3 feet (80 cm–1 m) apart.

Picea abies 'Nidiformis' is a flat-topped, horizontally branched spruce which, if planted closely enough, will give quite a good and unusual ground cover. It grows about 12 inches (30 cm) high and about 2 feet (60 cm) across, and should be spaced at around 18 inches (45 cm).

Taxus baccata 'Corley's Coppertip', a semi-prostrate yew, has green needles banded in creamy white which are bright copper when the new growth emerges in spring. It is about 12 inches (30 cm) tall and spreads to about 3 feet (1 m). It should be spaced at 2-foot (60-cm) intervals or a little closer. *T. baccata* 'Repens Aurea' is a golden, prostrate yew with a spread slightly wider than that of 'Coppertip'. Space plants about 2½ feet (80 cm) apart. *T. baccata* 'Summergold' is another semi-prostrate yew, which grows about as tall as 'Coppertip' but spreads to about 4½ feet (1.2 m). The foliage is especially vivid in summer.

The *tsuga* group of conifers contains some excellent low-growing types, such as 'Bennett', 'Cole' and 'Jeddeloh'. 'Cole' has the widest spread, up to 3 feet (1 m), but all three varieties are quite slow and need to be spaced about 18 inches (45 cm) apart if they are to achieve reasonable coverage in a year or two.

Herbaceous plants

As already mentioned on page 15, herbaceous perennials (including

---

A view of the 'Cambark garden' at Notcutt's Garden Centre, Peterborough (designed by the author), showing a small ground cover planting of heathers

Newly planted *Euonymus fortunei* 'Emerald n' Gold' – note initial spacing and mulch of bark low, spreading types usually sold as 'alpines') do have their limitations as far as ground-cover efficiency is concerned. Unless they are evergreen – of course, a good many are – they can become invaded with weeds early or late in the season if there should be an exceptionally warm spring or autumn when the odd weed can start to grow before it is smothered. On a large scale this does not really matter, as eventually the competition will be too great for any invaders, but it can make the scheme in a smaller garden look quite unsightly for a while.

In general, herbaceous ground cover needs more maintenance than that created by the close planting of shrubs. Many species will need dead-heading, but even those which do not will require periodic tidying of the old leaves. On the other hand, totally different effects can be achieved with the use of herbaceous perennials planted in large groups of single varieties, and certainly one gets away from the feeling of sameness which is inclined to attach to shrub, and especially evergreen and conifer, ground-cover schemes. Perhaps the best plan is to combine the two types of planting, using very low maintenance shrubs in the more inaccessible areas like the back of a large border and herbaceous plants near the front where it is easier to give them some attention.

You will find that, in the main, pests and diseases such as mildew will be more active on the soft tissue of herbaceous perennials than on the tougher leaves and woody stems of the shrubs. Naturally, there will be many exceptions to this, but it is wise to keep an eye open for problems as they start to occur, tackling them with a general purpose combined insecticide and fungicide at the first signs. Slugs and snails, particularly, enjoy the shelter and food provided by many perennials, particularly hostas, and the area should be treated with bail or liquid slug killer as soon as the first nibbles appear; if you wait until the whole patch is stripped, the ground-cover effect will be lost.

Here are some of what I find to be the most effective and least demanding herbaceous plants for ground-cover situations. In most cases, the suggestions for maintenance are not absolutely essential, but will improve the appearance of the scheme and help to prevent a build-up of the kind of nasties which are encouraged when plants of this nature are allowed to 'do their own thing'.

Acaena is usually sold as an 'alpine', although those species vigorous enough to be considered for ground cover would be difficult

GROUND COVER FOR LARGE, OPEN AREAS

to control on a rockery or alpine bed. The two I find make the best smothering plants are 'Blue Haze', a vigorous, low-growing cultivar with blue-bronze foliage and reddish flower heads, and 'Copper Carpet', a newer variety with coppery leaves and greenish-red flowers, which is capable of rapid spread. Both are evergreen and require little or no maintenance, and should be spaced about 12 inches (30 cm) apart.

Ajuga is an accommodating genus of plants, thriving in all but the driest of conditions and capable of standing quite a lot of shade if there is some moisture. The best varieties for ground cover are *Ajuga reptans* and its cultivars 'Burgundy Glow' (wine-red variegated leaves), 'Purpurea' (purple leaves), 'Variegata' (cream and light green) and 'Metallica' (purple, very vigorous). All are evergreen and have blue flower spikes. The plants themselves grow close to the ground and spread by running stems; at each point where they root another rosette of leaves is formed, which produces more runners, and so on, rather like the strawberry. The flower spikes tend to look untidy when they have faded and the plants' appearance is improved if they are trimmed off. Ajuga is rather prone to infestation by greenfly and mildew infection, and I find a preventative spraying with an insecticide and fungicide 'cocktail' helps to stop the appearance being temporarily spoilt by these nuisances. Spacing is the same as for acaena.

Alchemilla mollis is an easily cultivated plant with quite large, apple-green leaves having slightly frilled edges and dainty sprays of sulphur-yellow flowers in summer. It will stand some shade and needs little maintenance except for removing the dead leaves from time to time. It is almost evergreen and the delicate-looking flowers provide an interesting contrast to some of the 'chunkier' ground-cover subjects. Space the plants at 12–inch (30–cm) intervals. It seeds readily so any gaps are soon filled.

***Arabis caucasica* 'Plena'**, a quick-growing, double white form of the well-known 'rockery' plant, resembles a white aubretia, with which it associates well as a mass planting. There are many named cultivars of aubretia in colours ranging from pale lilac to deep rose, but if you are going to require a lot of plants of either this or arabis, then it is a good idea (and quite easy) to grow your own from seed. Most seed companies recommend sowing the seed in a cool greenhouse, but I find it will germinate quite well if sown in trays of

THE BIG COVER-UP

Alchemilla mollis

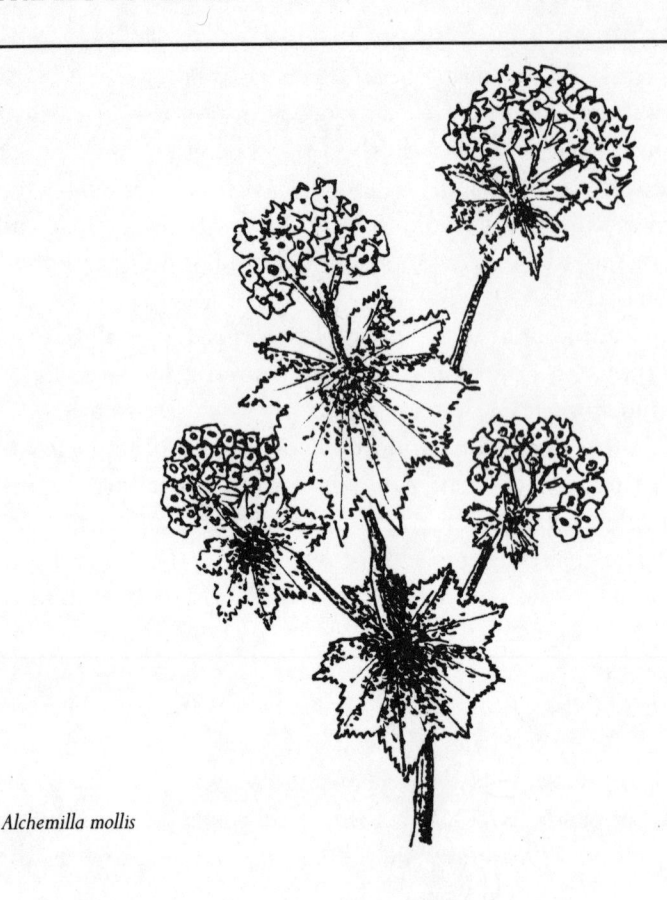

seed compost to which has been added a little sharp sand to make it more 'open', during late spring and summer. The plants should be big enough to plant out the following spring. Maintenance consists of cutting the plants back after flowering; if this is neglected, they tend to become bare and 'strawy' in the middle, and this tempts birds to remove large portions for nest-building. Established plants will also spread themselves by seed if the trimming is left until seed pods have formed and ripened. Spacing for both aubretia and arabis is 9 inches (20 cm) apart.

Bergenia (elephant's ears) is a popular plant with large, leathery leaves, which in some cultivars become red or purple-tinted in winter. Flower heads on stems roughly 18 inches (45 cm) long are produced in spring in colours ranging from white to deep red according to variety. Maintenance consists of the removal of old, shrivelled leaves periodically. The best varieties are 'Ballawley Hybrid' (rose flowers, red stems); *B. cordifolia* 'Purpurea' (carmine flowers,

GROUND COVER FOR LARGE, OPEN AREAS

deep red stems, purple leaves in winter); 'Bressingham Salmon'; 'Silver Light' (white flowers); 'Sunningdale' (reddish leaves, lilac carmine flowers). Space at 15–inch (38–cm) intervals.

Brunnera macrophylla has flowers like a forget-me-not, but it is quite perennial and has large, rough-textured, heart-shaped leaves. There is a much less strong-growing variegated-leaved form 'Variegata' with big cream splashes, and one with spotted leaves called 'Langtrees'. For ease of cultivation it is best to stick to *B. macrophylla* – this will also tolerate some shade. The variegated cultivar can scorch in very hot sunshine. Maintenance consists of clearing up the dead leaves occasionally. Spacing for *B. macrophylla* and 'Langtrees' is 12–15 inches (30–38 cm) apart, and for 'Variegata' 9 inches (20 cm) apart.

Campanula carpatica is low-growing, again usually sold as an 'alpine'. There are many good named varieties with large, bell-shaped

Campanula carpatica

flowers during summer. Once established, the plants spread rapidly and also seed themselves. Two similar low-growing species are *C. portenschlagiana* and *C. poscharskyana;* the latter can become quite invasive. No maintenance is necessary. Spacing for *C. carpatica* and *C. portenschlagiana* is 9–12 inches (20–30 cm); for *C. poscharskyana,* 12–15 inches (30–38 cm).

The attraction of **Dicentra spectabilis** (bleeding heart) for ground cover is its fern-like foliage and arching sprays of rosy-red, pink or white flowers in early summer. Once established, it is quite strong-growing and gives quite a cottage-garden feel to a cover-up scheme. Space the plants 15 inches (38 cm) apart.

An evergreen **spurge** which will thrive in most conditions, wet or dry, sun or shade, *Euphorbia robbiae* produces greenish-yellow flower heads in spring on top of stocky stems bearing rosettes of dark green evergreen leaves. It can become a nuisance as the plant itself is wide-spreading and every seed produced seems to germinate! Another spurge – not evergreen, unfortunately – which will cover large areas quickly is *E. griffithii* 'Fireglow', which has flame-red bracts in early summer, turning dark green. This plant needs tidying up during winter when the stems have died off. Perhaps the most striking of all herbaceous ground cover is *E. wulfenii,* another evergreen, with grey-green, willow-shaped leaves and unusual yellowish-green flowers in large heads on top of stems 2½–3 foot (80 cm–1 m) high. Maintenance is minimal with this plant, although until the individual specimens grow together and lend each other support, some temporary help may need to be given by way of brushwood or wire herbaceous plant supports. Space the plants 2½–3 feet (80 cm–1 m) apart.

The **hardy geraniums** (as opposed to the bedding geraniums, which are really pelargoniums) are easy to grow and make superb and colourful ground cover. Many varieties are suitable; it would be impossible to give a comprehensive list here, but the following are readily obtainable and entirely suitable. *Geranium endressii* 'Wargrave Pink' is an evergreen, with salmon-pink flowers. It grows to a height of about 18 inches (45 cm) when in flower, and blooms all summer. Space the plants 15 inches (38 cm) apart. An annual trim in spring keeps the plants neat. *G.* 'Johnson's Blue' spreads by suckers and produces bright blue flowers in June. It reaches a height of about 2 feet (60 cm) when in flower, and should be trimmed back after

GROUND COVER FOR LARGE, OPEN AREAS

flowering. Space at 18–inch (45–cm) intervals. *G. macrorrhizum* 'Walter Ingwersen' is semi-evergreen with soft pink flowers in early summer. The fragrant leaves take on good autumn colouring. The plant's height when in flower is 12 inches (30 cm); it should be spaced 12–15 inches (30–45 cm) away from its neighbour. *G.* × *magnificum* has violet-blue flowers all summer, when it reaches a height of 2 feet (60 cm). Space plants at 15–inch (38–cm) intervals.

G. procurrens is one of the best herbaceous ground-cover subjects there is, but it is not often seen. A low-growing, rapid carpeter 4 inches (10 cm) high, it flowers from June to November with deep magenta blooms. Plants should be spaced 1½–2 feet (45–60 cm) apart. Another magenta flowerer with a long season is *G. subcaulescens* 'Russell Prichard'. This variety has grey-green leaves and should be trimmed to keep it tidy. The plants grow to a height of 9 inches (20 cm) and should be spaced 12 inches (30 cm) apart. *G. sanguineum lancastriense* 'Splendens' produces spreading mats of evergreen foliage with bright pink flowers on 10–inch (25–cm) stems from June until the frosts. Trim the plants in spring if necessary to keep them in shape, and space them at 12–inch (30–cm) intervals.

Geums make broad clumps with thick foliage and have attractive, buttercup-shaped flowers early and again later in the summer. *Geum borisii* has strong orange single flowers, while *G. chiloense* 'Mrs. Bradshaw' is a double form with brick-red flowers. 'Lady Stratheden' has semi-double, deep yellow blooms. Geums should be cut down to ground level in the autumn, and will stand a certain amount of shade if it is not too heavy. Space plants 12 inches (30 cm) apart.

Glechoma hederacea 'Variegata' is better known as *Nepata hederacea* 'Variegata' and is usually found in garden centres at the beginning of summer being sold as a trailing bedding plant for window-boxes and hanging baskets. It is a variegated form of ground ivy often seen in hedge bottoms and has a characteristic strong scent when the leaves are crushed. It spreads by running stems producing rosettes of leaves which root where they touch the soil. Although the growth is rapid, the effect is sparse for a while until good coverage is achieved and so some hand weeding may be necessary. After that little maintenance is required and you may in fact experience difficulty in keeping the plant within bounds! Space individual plants 15–18 inches (38–45 cm) apart.

Heuchera sanguinea is an attractive border plant with evergreen,

THE BIG COVER-UP

saxifrage-like leaves (in fact, it is a member of the saxifrage family), and delicate-looking sprays of flowers on thin but wiry stems in midsummer. There are many varieties which are all suitable for ground-cover planting. The most easily obtainable are the 'Bressingham Hybrids' in mixed colours of reds and pinks. The flower stems are quite tall, growing up to 2½ feet (80 cm) high, and need to be cut off when the flowers have faded. 'Coral Cloud' produces coral-red sprays and is shorter, reaching about 2 feet (60 cm). There are also two green-flowered forms, 'Greenfinch' and its seedling, 'Green Ivory', which are also quite tall. Two more compact cultivars are 'Pretty Polly' (pink, 12 inches – 30 cm – high) and 'Shere Variety' (scarlet, 18 inches – 45 cm – tall). One variety which has become more readily available in recent years is 'Palace Purple', which has coloured leaves of warm purple which show off the small white flower sprigs well. Heuchera is a handy plant for the flower arranger and has few foibles, but it is unhappy if not planted deep enough, and sometimes has the tendency to become hard and woody at the base and work itself out of the soil. If this happens, the best plan is to dig the whole plant up and replant it deeper. Space them 12–15 inches (30–45 cm) apart.

Hostas have long been recommended as ground-cover plants, but if I have one criticism to make, it is that they tend to die and become mushy and messy in the autumn. This does not really matter where large areas are concerned, but if you are a tidiness fanatic or the site is in a prominent position, some clearing up will be necessary. There is a further snag in that hostas disappear from view completely in late October and do not reappear until spring, leaving some boring gaps in your ground-cover scheme. This can be overcome by interplanting with dwarf bulbs such as crocuses, scillas, chionodoxas, dwarf narcissi and species tulips. The dying and shabby foliage of these plants will in turn be adequately hidden by the developing leaves of the hostas as they reappear for the summer.

There are innumerable good new varieties of hostas available today, but some of them can be still quite expensive, and, as it is more than possible that you are going to need large quantities, it is wise to stick to some of the more common and less costly ones. Hostas have the reputation for liking moist shade, but in fact they are most accommodating plants as their thick root system will tolerate most locations. In fact, some of the golden and variegated-leaved cultivars will lose a lot of their colour unless they have a reasonable proportion of sunshine.

The larger-leaved hostas are the more efficient light-excluders, but some smaller, narrow-leaved hostas can let some light through to the ground and therefore not be entirely successful at the task in hand. The following is a small selection of names which you can expect to find without trouble and which ought to be at the less expensive end of the market. The list includes low, medium and tall growers for the front, middle and back of a planting. Where large stretches of ground are concerned, it is clearly more sensible to use plants with the widest spread.

Hosta fortunei has glaucous-blue leaves and lilac spikes of lily-shaped flowers in summer. The plant's height and spread are around 18 inches (75 cm), and it should be spaced 15–18 inches (38–45 cm) away from its neighbours. 'Aurea' is a slightly smaller form with yellowish foliage. 'Aureomarginata' has leaves edged with yellow and a habit similar to *H. fortunei*. 'Picta' resembles 'Aurea' but the young leaves are yellow and green. *H.* 'Golden Sunburst', an American

Hosta 'Honeybells'

import, is a vigorous, golden yellow form. In a really hot spot the leaves can scorch a little. Space the plants 18 inches (45 cm) apart. 'Honeybells' has green leaves and scented mauve flowers. It is a larger variety, with a height and spread of more than 2½ feet (80 cm), and should be spaced at 2-foot (60–cm) intervals. *H. lancifolia* is a moderate-growing, green-leaved form with plenty of flowers and a spread of 18 inches (45 cm). Plants should be spaced 15 inches (45 cm) apart.

H. rectifolia 'Tall Boy' has an upright habit, with large, dark green leaves. The violet flower spikes grow up to 4½ feet (1.2 m) high. Space plants 2 feet (60 cm) apart. 'Royal Standard', with very heavily scented white flowers, grows to 2½ feet (80 cm) in height. Spacing for these is at 2–foot (60–cm) intervals. *H. sieboldiana* has wide, crinkled leaves of a glaucous blue and pale lilac flowers. Plants grow 2 feet (60 cm) high and should be spaced 15 inches (38 cm) apart. *H. tardiana,* a dwarf hosta, useful for small pieces of ground and the front of borders, has blue leaves and almost white flowers on stems 15 inches (38 cm) tall. Spacing for these is 12 inches (30 cm) apart. *H.* 'Thomas Hogg' has a moderate habit, bright green leaves edged with white and mauve flowers. Space these plants 15–18 inches (38–45 cm) apart.

A golden form of creeping Jenny, **Lysmachia nummularia 'Aurea'** is a prostrate, rambling plant with yellow leaves and buttercup-yellow flowers in summer which spreads rapidly, rooting wherever the stems touch the earth, until it forms a weed-proof mat. The enthusiasm of the ordinary green form can become a nuisance, but the golden variety is slightly less invasive and the leaf colour alone brightens up an uninteresting piece of the garden. No attention is needed other than removing it from parts it has strayed into uninvited. Space the plants 15 inches (38 cm) apart.

All **mints** tend to overstretch the mark in a short time as their underground stems spread the plants far beyond the area in which they are required. However, *Mentha suaveolens* 'Variegata', the variegated form of pineapple mint, with its smallish, rounded and slightly furry leaves boldly marked with large patches of creamy-white, can be useful ground cover where something slightly different in form and texture is required. It is powerfully aromatic, especially when the weather is warm; the scent of the leaves is supposed to resemble that of a pineapple, but to me it can be rather too much of a good thing. It does not grow tall, maybe less than 18 inches (45 cm),

GROUND COVER FOR LARGE, OPEN AREAS

but the stems are rather lax and the whole thing can look untidy and straggly. However, if the plants are cut back once or twice a season they will become more bushy and able to stand up by themselves. Space the plants at intervals of 18 inches (45 cm) – or closer if you are in a real hurry.

Oreganum vulgare 'Aureum' is another aromatic herb which makes good ground cover, and is the golden form of wild marjoram, used in cooking as oregano. During the winter it is a low-growing, yellow-leaved plant, but in summer the golden-foliaged stems grow to about 12 inches (30 cm) or slightly more, and eventually produce mauve flower heads. The clumps spread fairly rapidly, but in late summer the planting can look tatty as the stems start to flop; however, this can be remedied by clipping the whole area over once or twice during the growing season. Space the plants 12 inches (30 cm) apart.

The **polygonum** genus contains some of the most invasive plants around, and several which, although not quite so rampant, one should think carefully about before including in a herbaceous border. They can, however, provide useful ground cover, and the unusual, drumstick like red or pink flower spikes contrast well with other massed plants.

Polygonum vacciniifolium is a most attractive plant, almost a sub-shrub, with vigorous prostrate growth covered in pink flowers from August to October. Like many other herbaceous ground cover candidates I have mentioned, it is usually to be found in the alpine section of catalogues and garden centres although, at the risk of repeating myself, I would think twice about putting it on my small rockery! *P. affine* will carpet an area rapidly, especially the cultivars 'Darjeeling Red' and 'Donald Lowndes', both of which reach about 12 inches (30 cm) when in flower. Many varieties of *P. affine* colour up well in the autumn. *P. bistortum* 'Superbum' a cultivated form of the native bistort or knotgrass is taller, up to 2½ feet (80 cm) high when in flower, with large, lush leaves where the soil is nice and moist. It has pink flowers like pokers and a longer than average flowering season.

P. campanulatum is a rather untidy plant, but does have its merits as far as ground cover is concerned. It spreads like wildfire where the soil is good, rather like some of the troublesome older varieties of golden rod. During the winter there is a partial coverage of leaves at

THE BIG COVER-UP

Polygonum bistortum 'Superbum'

ground level; in spring leafy stems sometimes reaching 3 feet (1 m) in height are produced, usually branching, and these eventually have rather loose heads of pink flowers for about two months during the height of summer. In open areas it may need some support at this stage. Spacing for *P. vacciniifolium* is 9–12 inches (20–30 cm), for *P. affine* 12 inches (30 cm), and for *P. campanulatum* 1½–2 feet (45–60 cm).

The **herbaceous potentillas** are quite different from the shrubby ones. They have leaves vaguely resembling a strawberry and flowers not dissimilar to the geum. Possibly the three best ground-cover varieties are 'Gibson's Scarlet', 'William Rollison' (a semi-double orange), and 'Yellow Queen', which has a particularly neat habit, but there are many other good cultivars about. These

GROUND COVER FOR LARGE, OPEN AREAS

three grow to between 12–18 inches (30–45 cm) and flower throughout the summer.

There are also several forms of dwarf herbaceous potentilla – again, usually found with the alpines – which do a satisfactory job of weed control where low-growing plants are required. One of these is *Potentilla alba,* which is about 4 inches (10 cm) tall, with emerald-green foliage and large white flowers with a yellow centre. *P. calabra* is also prostrate, with whitish-green foliage and yellow flowers. *P. tonguei* has trailing stems and buff and orange flowers. Maintenance of the dwarf species is usually negligible; the taller herbaceous varieties will need to have the dead heads and old stems removed at the end of the flowering season. Space the alpine forms 9–12 inches (20–30 cm) apart, and the standard varieties at intervals of 12–15 inches (30–38 cm).

Raoulia australis, another 'alpine', is a completely prostrate carpeter with mats of silvery-grey foliage. Plants need to be spaced 9–12 inches (20–30 cm) apart.

Saxifraga is yet another 'alpine', of which there are many cultivars in a wide selection of colours from pure white to deep red, with some nice yellows. The foliage is evergreen and the plants make ever-widening clumps, but have the annoying habit of dying out in patches, and, like aubretia and arabis, birds find the rather dry mature stems from the centre of the plants excellent nesting material, which does not help the overall effect. However, the results produced by a healthy mass planting of mossy saxifrages can be quite pleasing. Look for varieties like 'Pearly King', 'Flowers of Sulphur' and 'Triumph' (blood-red), which are all undemanding and reliable, and space plants 9 inches (20 cm) apart.

At this stage a strong word of warning will not come amiss. With many low-growing, and especially cushion-forming, plants, particularly those growing near to lawns which may be allowed to seed, there is a tendency for grass to germinate among the stems. It is wise to keep a sharp look-out for the first signs of young blades of grass among the foliage and either attempt to pull these out by the roots or, if they do not seem to want to come easily, a small dab of a systemic weedkiller such as Tumbleweed will 'nip them in the bud', so to speak, before they become too well established. How often do we see aubretia or mossy saxifrages almost hidden by grass which has been allowed to take over? Young grass is not too difficult to remove;

mature plants can be virtually impossible, and at this point the only answer is to dig out the whole area and start again. Many grasses, not just couch grass or twitch, have running rootstocks and can cover large areas in time. If you already have the problem, watering the plant and the grass with a solution of 'Weed-out', which claims to kill grassy-leaved species only, may help, but if the infestation is serious, several applications may be necessary and they may not be entirely successful, so in the long run still the only remedy is to dig everything up and replant.

The common form of **Sedum spurium** has slightly succulent leaves, a prostrate habit, and not unattractive, quite large heads of pink flowers in summer. It is an old cottage garden flower and most gardens usually have a patch or two somewhere, but it does make really good cover where it is allowed to develop fully. There are also some very nice cultivars available, again as 'alpines', and it may well be worth considering some of these for an area close to the property which is in view most of the time.

'Purple Carpet' has purple leaves and very bright pink flowers. The leaves of 'Variegatum' are variegated cream and green with wine tints. 'Erdblut' is green with carmine-red flowers. 'Green Mantle' has no flowers but makes very dense, bright green mats. You may find the appearance of the planting is improved by clipping over after flowering to trim off the dead heads. *S. spurium* dies back in winter, but there are usually signs of next year's shoots to be seen among the dormant stems. Space the plants 9–12 inches (20–30 cm) apart.

Tellima grandiflora **'Purpurea'** will grow well in some shade as well as in full sun and is a plant which most people recognize but few can put a name to. It is another one of the saxifrage family, and has leaves rather like heuchera, but they are hairy, and of a colour most sought after by flower arrangers: green-veined and purple, with an underside tinged wine-red. The flower spikes of pink-fringed green bells are also similar to heuchera. *T. grandiflora* is an evergreen, although the older leaves die off eventually and the plants look neater if they are removed. It spreads quite quickly as ever-widening clumps but never gets out of hand. Space at 12-inch (30-cm) intervals.

Tiarella cordifolia is similar to both heuchera (with which it has been crossed to give a pretty plant called heucherella, and this can also be used for smaller areas of ground cover) and tellima. It is also known as foam flower because of its feathery white fluffy flower

GROUND COVER FOR LARGE, OPEN AREAS

spikes. The leaves are evergreen, making it quite efficient as a weed suppressor, and vaguely heart-shaped, often turning a pleasant bronzy colour in winter. Spacing is the same as for tellima.

Dwarf creeping **thymes** come into the same category as raoulia as far as ground cover is concerned. They are handy for covering ground at the edge of a bed or border, and if they are allowed to spill over on to the path they can be walked on without detriment and will smell very good. There are many varieties to choose from. 'Anderson's Gold' retains its bright golden colour all winter, *Thymus herba-barona* smells of caraway, and *T. micans* has very dark foliage and pink flowers. *T. serpyllum* is perhaps the best known creeping thyme, and has a white form ('Albus'), several red ones, like T. 'Coccineus' and 'Coccineus Major', and some good pinks, for example 'Annie Hall' and 'Pink Chintz'. Plants should be spaced 9 inches (20 cm) apart.

Veronica prostrata is, as one would imagine, a prostrate form of the herbaceous veronica. Most cultivars are blue, like 'Blue Sheen', 'Loddon Blue', 'Spode Blue' and 'Waterperry Blue', but there is a pretty pink form, 'Mrs Holt', although this is less strong-growing and needs to be planted closer together than the others, which should be planted at intervals of 9–12 inches (20–30 cm).

Bamboos and grasses

Grass is, of course, a first-class and perhaps the most widely planted form of ground cover – certainly in this country. The density of growth of suitable species is such that few invaders are allowed to become established as long as the growth is healthy. The main reason why our lawns become sparse and weed-infested is wrong cultivation and over-zealousness with the mower without adequate replenishment of lost nutrients by way of regular fertilizing.

Bamboos are also members of the grass family, and have a running habit which makes them ideal for filling up large areas while keeping other intruders at bay. Some can grow too tall for this section, although I will be mentioning them later on in the book, but there are some moderate growers which are worth considering.

As far as the proper grasses are concerned, they can suppress weeds either by creeping rootstocks or because they form dense clumps. My remarks concerning cushion-forming dwarf perennials (see page 47) apply equally well here: if unwanted species are allowed to get mixed up in the planting it is usually quite impossible to get rid

THE BIG COVER-UP

Arundinaria viridistriata

of them. You cannot even use a selective weedkiller, as what will work on one type of grass will also work on the type you want to retain.

Bamboos
Arundinaria variegata has slim stems which grow to about 3 feet (1 m) and long, dark green leaves with creamy white stripes. The habit is tufted but the clumps widen quickly and coverage is rapid. Space the plants 2 feet (60 cm) apart. *A. viridistriata* grows taller, up to 4 feet (1.2 m) high, with purple canes and leaves variegated green and gold. *A. pumila*, *A. pygmaea* and *A. vagans* are dwarf, wide-spreading, carpeting species, and need to be spaced 2½–3 feet (80 cm–1 m) apart.

Sasa are thicket-forming bamboos. *Sasa veitchii*, also known as *S.*

GROUND COVER FOR LARGE, OPEN AREAS

albomarginata or *Arundinaria veitchii,* is a fine ground-cover plant with large leaves which develop white, straw-like margins in winter. Spacing is the same as above. *S. tessellata* grows much taller, and has very large, shiny leaves. It grows into dense thickets, with bright green, slender canes which arch over. Plants should be spaced 3–4 feet (1–1.2 m) apart.

Grasses

Agropyron magellanicum has clumps of silver-blue foliage, and grows to a height of about 12 inches (30 cm). Space the plants 12 inches (30 cm) apart.

With its blue-grey foliage and graceful flowering heads in early summer, *Avena candida* grows to an overall height of 18 inches (45 cm). It should be planted at 15–inch (38–cm) intervals.

Carex morrowii 'Evergold', a low-growing ornamental grass, reaches only about 9 inches (20 cm) in height. It has arching leaves striped green and gold, and should be spaced at 12–inch (30–cm) intervals.

Most varieties of pampas grass are too big to be considered as ground-cover candidates except where there is unlimited space, but *Cortaderia selloana* 'Pumila' is more compact, and even when bearing plumes the overall height is less than 6 feet (2 m). The dense leaves make weed invasion virtually impossible. As with all grasses, an annual tidying up is desirable, but it is unwise to set fire to the old foliage in spring as in dry seasons some damage can occur to the roots. Space plants 4 feet (1.2 m) apart.

Festuca glauca is a low-growing, wiry grass of a pleasant blue-grey colour, while F. alpina is a green form. The two contrast well and should be planted 12 inches (30 cm) apart.

Hakonechloa macra albo-aurea is an unusual Japanese grass. It is green and variegated buff with bronze tints. This grass grows to a height of 10 inches (25 cm), and plants should be spaced 9 inches (20 cm) apart.

Molinia caerulea 'Variegata' is a neat variegated grass which grows about 18 inches (45 cm) high. It is much more suitable for use as ground cover than that invasive grass *Phalaris picta* (gardeners' garters), which is almost as big a nuisance as couch grass, especially in light, sandy soils, and should only be planted in this kind of situation as a last resort. Spacing for *Molinia caerulea* 'Variegata' is at intervals of 1½–2 feet (45–60 cm).

Spartina pectinata 'Aureo-marginata' is a graceful grass, reaching

THE BIG COVER-UP

about 4 feet (1.2 m) when in flower. Space plants 2 feet (60 cm) apart.

The 'gigantea' of *Stripa gigantea* refers to the large, feathery flower spikes rather than the grass itself, which grows less than 3 feet (1 m) tall, even when in flower. Plant at intervals of 1½–2 feet (45–60 cm).

The foregoing is by no means a complete list of all species suitable for compact, open ground cover, but in my experience it embraces most of the more successful ideas. However, as I said earlier, the object of ground cover is to cover the ground thereby making life easier for cultivation, and there are many things I have not mentioned which would do the job with equal success, including black polythene and concrete!

Ground cover for partially shaded areas, including dappled shade under trees

There are many occasions in a garden when you would wish to use ground cover but the area is not in sun for the whole or greater part of the day. By far the commonest example is the ground on the edge of mature deciduous trees and larger shrubs, where the sun is filtered through their leaves, causing a dappled effect welcomed by many plants otherwise prone to drying out or scorching in totally open situations.

Partial shade can also be provided by low buildings, walls, fences and similar constructions which screen the ground near them for more than half of the day, especially when the structure prevents the warmer south and west sun from reaching the plants.

There are many plants suitable for use in ground-cover schemes in this kind of location which are just as good-looking and untemperamental as the ones already described. The main thing is to get the planting conditions exactly right. Where the area is shaded by a man-made structure, no additional cultivation (other than that which you would give any part of the garden before installing long-lived and not inexpensive plants) is necessary, but where the site is at the edge of trees, you could have a problem with insufficient water reaching the plants, especially as they are getting established, because the canopy may shield the ground from rain when the wind is in a certain direction, and also some trees have very far-reaching root systems, and these will also want their share of any available soil moisture.

It is important, therefore, that as much water-retaining material as possible in the way of organic matter is worked in prior to planting; not only will this help to retain water but it will also improve the texture of the soil so that the plants can get off to a good start and become established in the shortest time possible.

Plants in this sort of situation will also need extra attention to watering in dry spells, especially for the first couple of summers or so after planting. However, areas which are shaded by solid, non-living structures are likely to lose less moisture, and so should be easier to look after than sites in full sun.

Once light levels begin to be reduced in these ways, the choice of plants with bright flowers is reduced, but to compensate for this, many variegated plants actually look better as the non-green areas are not damaged by hot sun, and there are also some flowers, often those with red or orange coloration, which retain their colour more satisfactorily as they will not be bleached as much by the sun.

Low-growing evergreen shrubs for partially shaded areas

The evergreen forms of **berberis** which are suitable as ground cover have already been described on pages 18–19, and all those mentioned will grow well in partial shade, but it must be remembered that where the area is likely to be affected by large amounts of leaves falling on to it in autumn, and you want to keep the planting tidy by clearing them up, the job can be most unpleasant unless you are wearing thick gloves and thornproof trousers. When the scheme is in its early stages, you can neaten it up in autumn by digging the leaves in, but as the plants close up you will not be able to do this easily, and there still remains the question of what you do about those leaves which have settled among the branches of the berberis themselves. Perhaps, all things considered, berberis are not the wisest choice for this kind of situation. The same comment applies to deciduous berberis, but because the leaves are renewed every year, they do tend to cover up the debris nestling in the heart of the shrub more efficiently.

The **cotoneasters** listed on pages 19–21 will stand quite dense shade, but the totally prostrate ones are hard to tidy up where they are planted under trees, because you cannot rake up the leaves without the branches being pulled by the rake, which often causes them to split or snap off. They are, however, excellent for other partially and totally shaded areas.

Euonymus fortunei varieties are impervious to shade unless it is of the heaviest, and so are quite appropriate for the sort of positions we are looking at in this chapter. The colour is just as good on the variegated forms in partial shade as it is in full sunlight, but in the case of the all-green kinds which turn purplish in autumn and winter,

GROUND COVER FOR PARTIALLY SHADED AREAS

I do find that this can be affected if the light is reduced more than a certain amount. Where the plants are growing in the vicinity of much taller things, the bushes may eventually become rather straggly, but this can be remedied by cutting them back quite hard every other year in spring.

Hebe **'Carl Teschner'** will withstand partial shade without any change, but the flowering can be affected if the sun is excluded for the greater part of the day.

In my garden *Lonicera nitida* **'Baggensen's Gold'** (see page 24) is planted at the edge of an old apple tree and keeps its colour well, but during the summer, when the canopy of apple tree leaves is at its thickest, I find that it needs clipping regularly to encourage plenty of juvenile growth, which is the brightest. There is a very successful planting of this shrub on a site in a town near me which does not receive any sun from late morning in summer, and much less, of course, in winter.

Osmanthus delaveyi makes a rounded shrub about 3 feet (1 m) across with a dense covering of small, leathery, dark green leaves giving very dense cover. The flowers are smallish, white and tubular with a heavy scent and are produced early in the year, around April. In the very coldest parts of Britain some frost damage may occur in bad seasons, but it is not particularly warm where I live and I have never had any trouble with it, especially when close-planted as ground cover, as the individual bushes tend to give protection to each other. No pruning is necessary. Space the plants 2½ feet (80 cm) apart.

Pachysandra terminalis is a low-growing shrub, more of a sub-shrub really, which reaches less than 9 inches (20 cm) in height but spreads by suckering stems to form wide clumps in time. It is a good ground-cover plant for smaller areas as it does not romp away, but always remains tidy. *P. terminalis* 'Variegata' is variegated with creamy-grey which grows more slowly, but is more interesting. *P. terminalis* is easily propagated by pieces of stem detached from the main plant with a few roots (what is technically known as an 'Irishman's cutting'). The flowers are greenish-white in late winter and early spring. *P. terminalis* will tolerate quite shady conditions but the variegated cultivar needs rather more light to produce good leaf colour. 'Variegata' can be grown in full sun, but the green type is inclined to scorch if planted in

THE BIG COVER-UP

too sunny a position. Plants should be spaced 12–15 inches (30–38 cm) apart.

Skimmia, an attractive family of small evergreens, has one drawback: on very chalky and alkaline soils the plants become chlorotic, and in very severe cases the leaves, especially those most recently produced, can be almost white. This affects the food-making functions and the plants gradually weaken. A temporary remedy is to water the soil in the area with sequestrene which will provide iron and other trace elements in a form which is not 'locked up' by the lime in the soil. Unfortunately, this treatment has to be repeated annually, which is a costly and not entirely satisfactory business, so perhaps the best advice is that, where your soil is known to have a pH of more than 7, you should avoid planting skimmia, though you do not need to have such acid conditions as if you were using, say, rhododendrons or summer-flowering heathers.

Apart from the hermaphrodite *Skimmia reevesiana,* which is a very small, choice shrub, but not strong of constitution and generally expensive to buy (and so not a particularly good candidate as a ground-cover shrub), all skimmias are either male or female. The best male form is *S. rubella,* which has red winter buds opening to pink heads of very sweetly scented flowers in early spring. Another good

Skimmia rubella

GROUND COVER FOR PARTIALLY SHADED AREAS

male form is *S. laureola*. This has larger leaves than *S. rubella* which have a very pungent smell when crushed. The flowers are white and also have a strong scent. The female species bear bright red berries; *S. japonica* has a dense habit, small leaves and medium-sized berries. The cultivar 'Foremanii' has larger leaves and berries. Skimmias do not need to be pruned. Space the plants 15–18 inches (38–45 cm) apart, and plant three females to one male if you want berries.

I have already recommended **Stranvaesia davidiana 'Prostrata'** as ground cover for open areas, but it will do equally well in partial shade. However, the remarks about the prostrate forms of cotoneaster (page 54) apply to this plant also: rough handling when clearing up leaves under and near trees can damage the trailing branches, though *S. davidiana* 'Prostrata' is a good shrub for any other type of partial shade, and will even stand full shade if it is not too dense. If the part of the garden you are thinking of using it in is known to be a frost pocket it might be wise to choose something else; the younger plants can be quite seriously affected during the extremes of a cold winter.

Viburnum davidii is a low-growing species of viburnum with large, very dark green, heavily-veined evergreen leaves, which grows into a dense mound about 2½ feet (80 cm) high by 4½ feet (1.5 m) in diameter. Like skimmia, male and female flowers are carried on separate plants, but unlike skimmia, the males do not differ from the females, except for the reproductive parts. Close grouping of plants, with a proportion of male forms, should ensure the production of unusual, turquoise-blue berries after the clusters of white flowers in June. Again, no pruning is necessary. Space plants 2½–3 feet (80 cm–1 m) apart.

Vinca is variously described as a trailing shrub, sub-shrub or herbaceous perennial depending on which catalogue you look it up in. The plain green form of *Vinca major* – the greater periwinkle – is unlovely and only suitable for really tough situations. There is a variegated cultivar which is slightly more pleasant but can still get untidy and out of hand if it is not clipped back regularly, but the blue flowers are pretty. A more unusual form of greater periwinkle is *V. major* 'Maculata' which has more discreet variegations: a central splash of sulphur yellow, shading into the green edges, rather like the large-leaved ivy 'Paddy's Pride'. This form is good for flower arranging as the foliage is more subtle.

THE BIG COVER-UP

Viburnum davidii

In light shade the lesser periwinkles (*V. minor*) make a good, quite prostrate cover and are less sprawling, though they can cover quite a distance in time, and periodically new plants are formed where the growing tips touch the ground, so coverage will become quite thick in a number of years. The species has bright blue flowers with the best flush in spring and early summer, but some flowers are produced throughout the summer until mid-autumn depending on season. 'Atropopurea' has plum-purple flowers; in 'Multiplex' these are double. 'Variegata' and 'Aureo-variegata' have blue flowers and cream and gold variegated leaves respectively. There is a white-flowered, variegated form, and also one with white flowers and green leaves called 'Gertrude Jekyll'. 'Bowles' Variety' has very large blue flowers, and 'Azurea Flore Pleno' has double ones. Pruning, by clipping over periodically, is more for the sake of appearance than anything else. Plant *V. minor* 12 inches (30 cm) apart and *V. major* at intervals of 15 inches (38 cm).

Low-growing deciduous shrubs for partial shade
Deciduous varieties of berberis can be planted in partial shade, but see the note on page 54.

Hypericum androsaemum **(tutsan),** is a semi-woody native shrub with rosettes of smallish yellow flowers followed by heads of black berries. The foliage is semi-evergreen in sheltered spots and mild winters and the bushes spread quite quickly but look better if they are cut back periodically as they can begin to look woody and straggly. Space plants 2 feet (60 cm) apart.

Most **shrubby potentillas** will tolerate zshade providing the sun reaches them for at least a short time during the day in summer, but as the amount of sunshine decreases, so does the abundance of flower. However, the more unusual coloured potentillas, with red, pink or orange flowers, such as 'Red Ace', 'Royal Flush', 'Princess', 'Tangerine' and 'Sunset' will keep their colour much better when not scorched by the full force of the sun.

Chaenomeles speciosa, the Japanese quince, will flower just as well in partial shade as in direct sunshine, but the season tends to be delayed a week or two. Apart from 'Simonii', the cultivars 'Moeloesii' (apple blossom pink on the outside and white on the inside of the flowers) and 'Umbilicata' are also good for ground cover candidates.

C. × superba are hybrids with a dense, rounded habit rather than the spreading one of *C. speciosa,* and make good cover where the space is more confined. This group contains some old favourites – 'Crimson and Gold', 'Knaphill Scarlet', 'Pink Lady' and 'Rowallane' (crimson) – which require little regular attention once established. Where you are working to a budget, you could consider planting *C. japonica,* an inexpensive, low, spreading, thorny shrub up to 3 feet (1 m) high, which has a profusion of red flowers followed by edible 'quinces' when mature. Space the plants 3 feet (1 m) apart.

Those **dwarf willows** with woolly leaves, such as *Salix lanata,* really need quite a lot of sun to do their best, but there are one or two smaller species which will tolerate some shade. The Kilmarnock willow, *S. caprea* 'Pendula', is one of these. Usually seen as a small, weeping tree grafted onto a single trunk, it can be grown as a low, spreading shrub on its own roots, when it makes a wide, hummocky bush, which is particularly attractive in spring when covered in yellow and grey 'pussy' catkins. They need to be spaced 4 feet (1.2 m) or more apart. A rare, carpet-forming willow sometimes seen is *S.* × *cottetii*, which also has catkins in early spring before the leaves. Spacing is the same as for *S. caprea*. *S. hastata* 'Wehrhahnii' is an upright-branched shrub but the bush itself has a spreading habit. It eventually reaches about 4 feet (1.2 m) in height and has a great many grey catkins in spring. These should be planted at intervals of 3 feet (1 m). Pruning is only necessary when the planting begins to get out of hand.

All the dwarf forms of spiraea will stand some shade, but those with golden leaves will not be as brightly coloured where the light levels are too low. However, I have a group of 'Golden Princess' at the edge of the canopy of my old apple tree which is just as well coloured as those in a more open part of the garden.

Conifers

In the main, conifers do not like shaded positions, though if the shade is only during part of the day, and preferably not under the drip of trees, most prostrate forms of juniperus (including those listed between pages 30 and 35) will put up quite a good show. Where it is overhung by trees, ground cover planting of junipers is usually more successful when the tree and the cover grow up together. If you try to establish conifers under well-grown trees you have the problem of dryness at the roots and also a possible shortage of nutrients, and these two factors will conspire to get the young bushes off to a bad start. As there are so many other things which do thrive in this kind of situation, it makes more sense to consider these first, only using junipers if you have some overriding desire to plant them in preference to more suitable subjects. If the two grow up together, the ground-cover conifers can become well established before being placed under threat by the tree; in any case, it will take many years before a sapling begins to have a detrimental effect on them, by which time it may seem in order to clear the whole lot out and redevelop that part of the garden, using the mature trees as a basis.

GROUND COVER FOR PARTIALLY SHADED AREAS

It is pointless to plant expensive cultivars in areas affected by trees, although in other shaded places it is really up to you whether you opt for the top or the bottom end of the price bracket. The best conifers for situations where they are almost certain to be stressed are the all-green, strong-growing forms like *Juniperus repanda, J. horizontalis, J. procumbens, J. tamariscifolia,* and even *J. pfitzeriana,* which will make a much smaller bush when growing in competition with trees.

Herbaceous plants tolerant of partial shade

Ajuga (see page 37) will withstand quite a lot of shade, but I find that some of the purple forms seem to be more prone to mildew in a situation which is not in full sun, and therefore need to be watched much more carefully for the disease.

Alchemilla mollis is quite happy in shade, even under trees, and will continue to seed itself quite readily. See page 17 for cultivation and spacing.

Bergenia will stand shade if the position is quite open, but it does not care to be crowded and overhung by larger plants as it will go straggly, the leaves will become smaller, and those that colour up in winter are more likely to remain green. Space at 15–inch (38–cm) intervals.

Brunnera macrophylla will grow in full shade, again if the position is uncluttered. 'Langtrees' and especially 'Variegata' prefer some sunlight to assist the variegations on the leaves. In my garden, 'Variegata', after taking a while to become established, now grows well in the dappled sunlight cast by a birch tree some yards away. Details of cultivation and spacing are found on page 39.

Dicentra spectabilis (page 40) will thrive in half-shade, but if the plant receives no sun at all it grows floppy and unhappy-looking. Plants should be spaced 15 inches (38 cm) apart.

Euphorbia robbiae will spread rapidly almost anywhere, but in my opinion can look rather sombre when out of flower. However, if it is planted to contrast with lighter coloured foliage – say, *Pachysandra terminalis* 'Variegata' - the effect can be quite eye-catching. (See page 55 for spacings.) The other euphorbias mentioned on page 40 prefer full sun, but there are one or two non-evergreen forms which spread quite well and like light shade. One is the semi-evergreen *E. amygdaloides rubra,* a wood spurge with red shoots and leaves which become darker as the season progresses, and sulphur-yellow flower

Bergenia 'Silver Light'

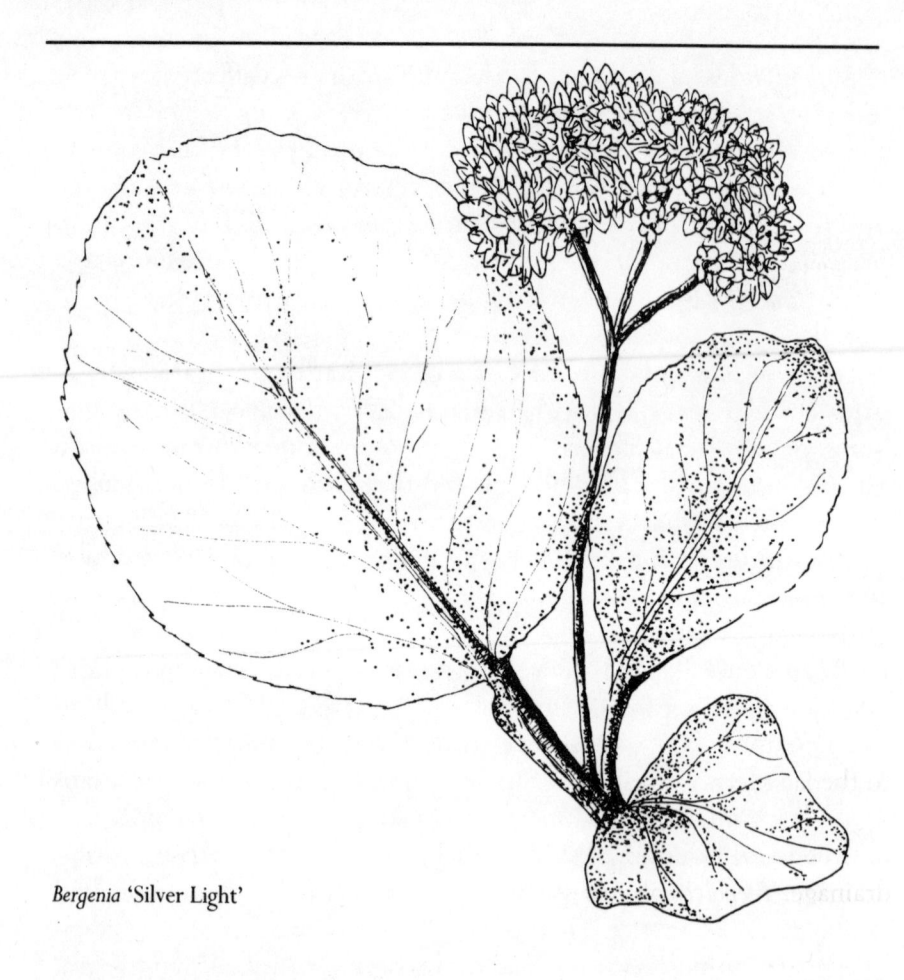

heads in early summer. The plant can grow about 2 feet (80 cm) tall in flower. Once established it, too, will spread by means of seed. *E. polychroma* dies down in winter, but spreads quickly in light soil to give a good summer coverage. The yellow early summer flowers are pleasant, and if you find the stems becoming rather floppy you can always cut the plants back to ground level and they will put on another flush of growth. The height is similar to or slightly shorter than *E. amygdaloides rubra,* and spacings for both are about 15 inches (38 cm) apart.

There are many species of **epimedium** which all make good ground cover. *E. perraldenianum* is possibly the most adaptable and will grow virtually anywhere, but it is inclined to die out if overcrowded with denser plants. The creeping roots produce long-stalked, nearly evergreen leaves and bright yellow, dainty sprays of flowers on

GROUND COVER FOR PARTIALLY SHADED AREAS

12-inch (30-cm) stalks in late spring. *E. cantabrigensis* has brownish-orange flowers; *E. macranthum* is pale pink; *E. rubrum* has reddish flowers; and *E. youngianum* 'Niveum' is a good ivory white. *E. versicolor* 'Sulphureum' is an excellent foliage variety, which colours well in spring and autumn and is another semi-evergreen, with a bonus of pale yellow flowers. Space plants 12 inches (30 cm) apart for quick coverage, otherwise at intervals of 15 inches (38 cm).

Not all **ferns** make good ground cover, but there are some which do, and where the area is shaded and fairly cool, they could well be considered along with flowering plants. *Asplenium scolopendrium*, the hart's-tongue fern, is one of these, and as it does not grow more than 12-18 inches (30-45 cm) high, it looks quite neat. It has green, tongue-like leaves, which are retained for most of the winter, but the plants benefit from an annual cutting back in spring to remove the old, tatty growth. Space plants 15 inches (38 cm) apart. *Athyrium filis-femina*, the lady fern, is a British native with lacy, bright green fronds up to 2½ feet (80 cm). This fern should be spaced 18 inches (45 cm) apart. *Dryopteris filix-mas*, the male fern, is another useful species for mass planting, and requires similar conditions and spacing to the lady fern.

Polystichum has several species suitable for light shade. *P. aculeatum* has leathery fronds up to 3 feet (1 m) long, and requires good drainage. *P. polyblepharum* is evergreen, growing to about 18 inches (45 cm) high. *P. setiferum*, the soft shield fern, is another taller-growing British native. A shorter form is *P. setiferum divisilobum*, which is also leathery, the fronds being finely divided. All these species should be spaced 18-24 inches (45-60 cm) apart according to budget and patience.

Fragaria alpina* (alpine strawberry) is easily raised from seeds and makes an attractive and evergreen ground cover with the benefit of small, sweet edible fruit as well. Space plants 9-12 inches (20-30 cm) apart. There is also an ornamental strawberry with leaves variegated with streaks and splashes of white, which has little, hard, inedible fruits and, like the alpine variety, quickly establishes itself on a piece of ground by means of runners. This plant is variable in its markings, and can often revert to all-green, which is disappointing as it does not have a lot going for it apart from the variegations. Space plants 12-15 inches (30-38 cm) apart.

The **geraniums** described on pages 40-41 are adaptable

regarding shade requirements, and so can be used for ground cover even where there is only a little sunshine during the day. Another species which is also worth planting (don't be put off by the depressing name!) is *Geranium phaeum,* the mourning widow, which is a strong grower with purple flowers; there is a white form, 'Album'. It grows to about 2 feet (60 cm) in height and requires spacing at 18–inch (45–cm) intervals.

I have listed **variegated ground elder** (*Aegopodium podagraria* 'Variegatum') under its common name as I think it is more likely that you will recognize it by this than its mouthful of a Latin name! The very mention of the dreaded weed, ground elder, might prevent you considering this plant, but it really does have its uses, and looks quite nice, the leaves (which in all other respects resemble ordinary ground elder) being well variegated with cream. The method of spreading itself, by means of underground running rhizomatomous roots, is also similar to ordinary ground elder, though it is not as rampant. It is easy to establish in sun or shade, provided the shade is not too dark, and soon forms a good cover. The drawback is that it is not evergreen, exposing bare earth in winter, and it is difficult to underplant with bulbs as they will eventually be choked by the roots. It is wise to choose the position of this plant with care, as it knows no boundaries, but you can buy one plant to start with, and by the end of the season you will have enough material to fill quite a large area, so it is very easy on the pocket. Just make sure that you will never want to remove it, especially if your soil is heavy! Initial spacing is 15–18 inches (38–45 cm) apart; more if you are economizing.

Helleborus orientalis (Lenten rose) looks rather like the more widely recognized Christmas rose, *H. niger,* but it grows taller and I find it easier to cultivate. It is usually obtained as seedlings, as it is easy to grow from seed, although there are some superb named varieties – but these are most costly. The flowers come out in spring, and range in colour from greenish-white to a deep maroon. *H. orientalis* requires little attention if it is given good growing conditions to start with, and will self-seed once established. Space plants 12–15 inches (30–38 cm) apart.

H. foetidus (stinking hellebore) is a nasty name for a nice plant, which grows wild in some parts of Britain and is widespread in gardens. It has dark-green, cut-leaved foliage and heads of pale lemon bells rimmed with maroon in early spring. This also seeds well and is

GROUND COVER FOR PARTIALLY SHADED AREAS

Lenten rose

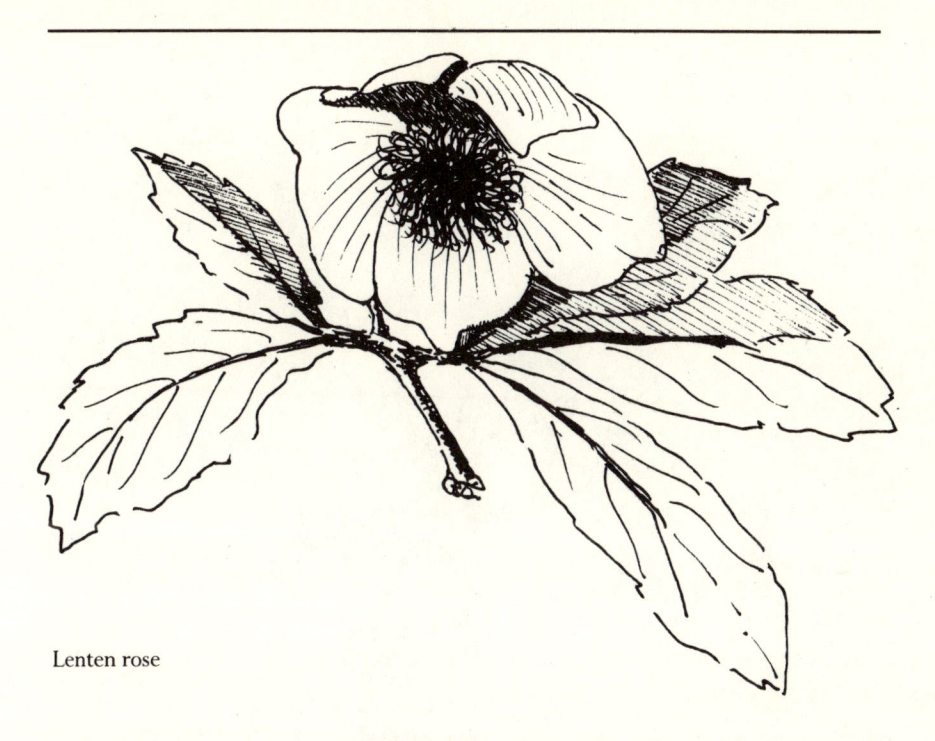

quite evergreen. Space at 15–inch (38–cm) intervals. At 2 feet (60 cm), *H. corsicus* (Corsican hellebore) is taller, and has leathery, less finely-cut leaves with big heads of apple-green flowers later in the spring. If the clumps start to look untidy, they can be cut down as new growth will come from the middle. *H. corsicus* also self-seeds, making quite thick cover in time. Initial spacing is 18–24 inches (45–60 cm) apart.

Hostas have already been described in some detail on pages 42–44. There are no varieties of these useful plants which I have had experience of that will not grow in light shade, and there are a few, like 'Sun Power' (a wavy-leaved yellow), and *Hosta undulata* 'Medio-variegata', another smaller-growing type, which scorch quite badly in too hot a position, so are admirably suitable for this kind of situation, and brighten it up, too. Space plants at about 12–inch (30–cm) intervals.

Iris foetidissima, the stinking iris, which smells unpleasantly rather like burning rubber if cut or damaged in any way, is another British native. The evergreen, dark leaves are nothing to write home about, but the small, bluish-violet early summer flowers have a gentle charm, and the plant is worth growing for the seed heads, which split

THE BIG COVER-UP

Iris foetidissima

open in autumn to reveal rows of bright orange seeds which germinate easily. Space these plants 15 inches (38 cm) apart for best effect. There is a variegated form which is less strong-growing and takes a long time to form clumps of any decent size, so it is not really suitable as a ground-cover plant for any appreciable area.

The **dead nettles** are invaluable for giving quick and colourful coverage to a lightly, and, in some cases, more heavily, shaded spot. *Lamium galebdolon* 'Variegatum' is rather too rampant for all but the most difficult places (see page 75) but there is a cultivar 'Silver

---

Carex morrowii 'Evergold' – a dwarf grass that can be mass planted

Euphorbia 'Fireglow' is excellent cover for large areas

Potentilla 'Red Ace' (*top left, overleaf*) needs some protection from hot sun

Detail of aubretia flower (*top right, overleaf*)

Massed aubretia (*bottom right, overleaf*) will cover a sunny area or edge a rose border

Potentilla 'Abbotswood' (*bottom left, overleaf*) – cover for sunny ground

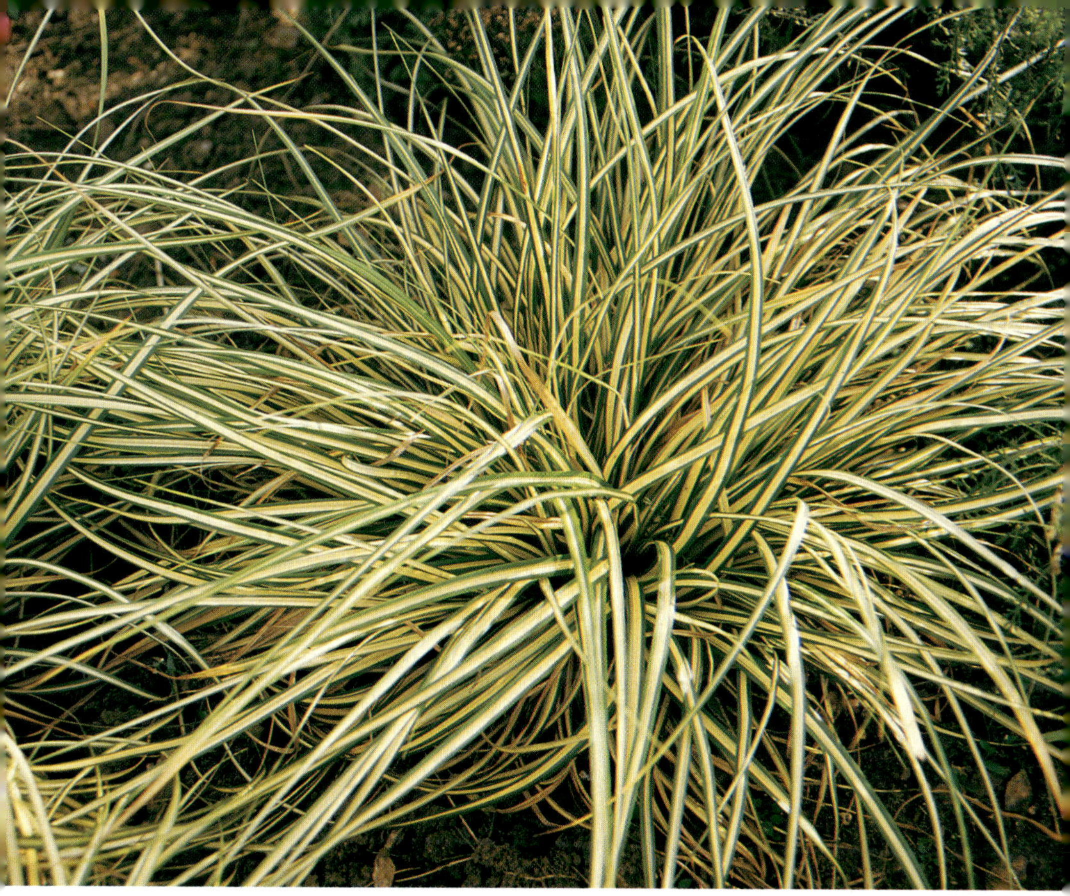

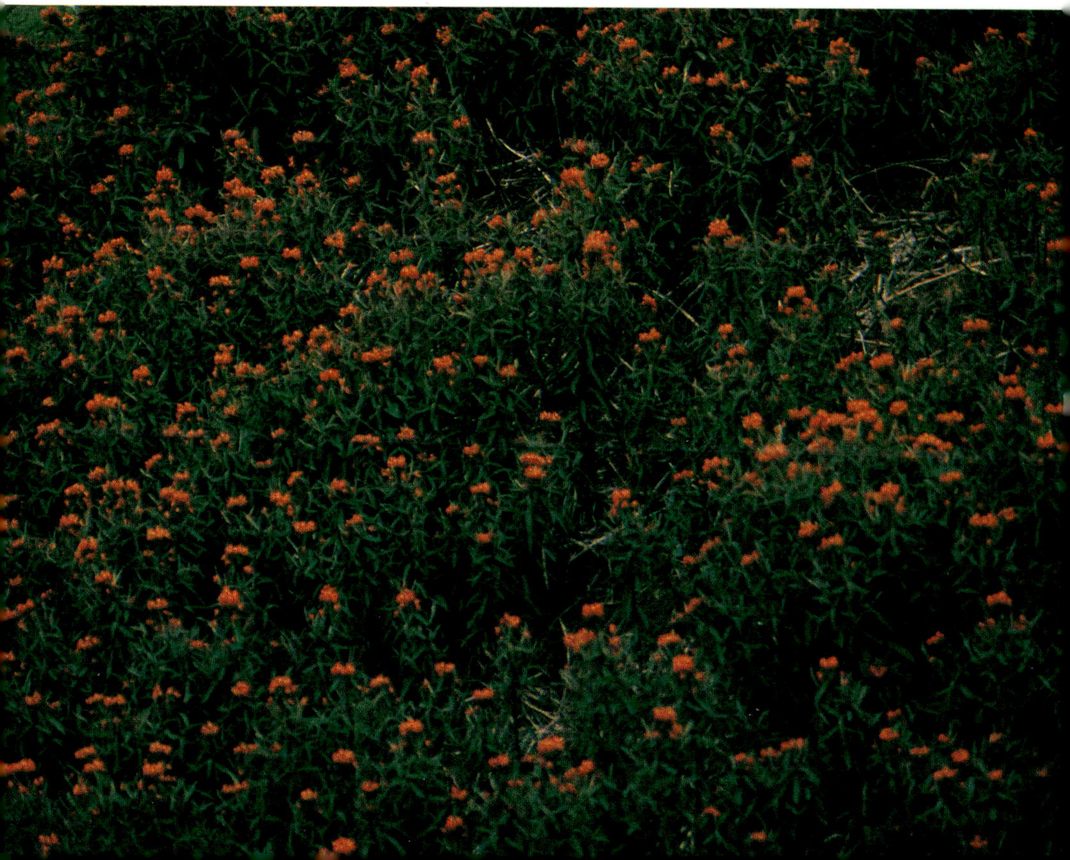

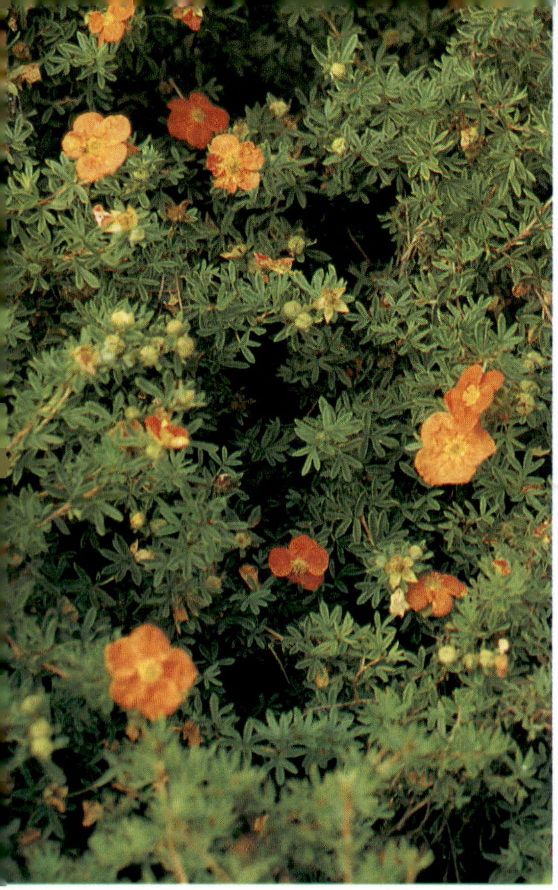
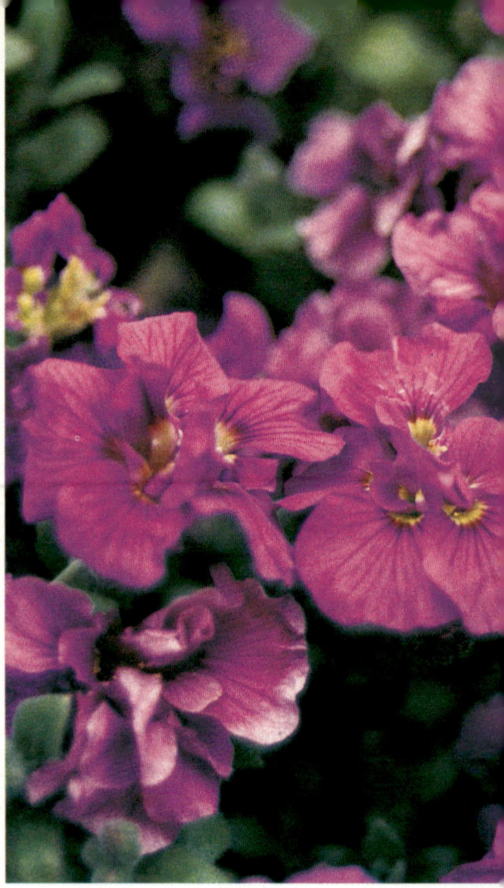
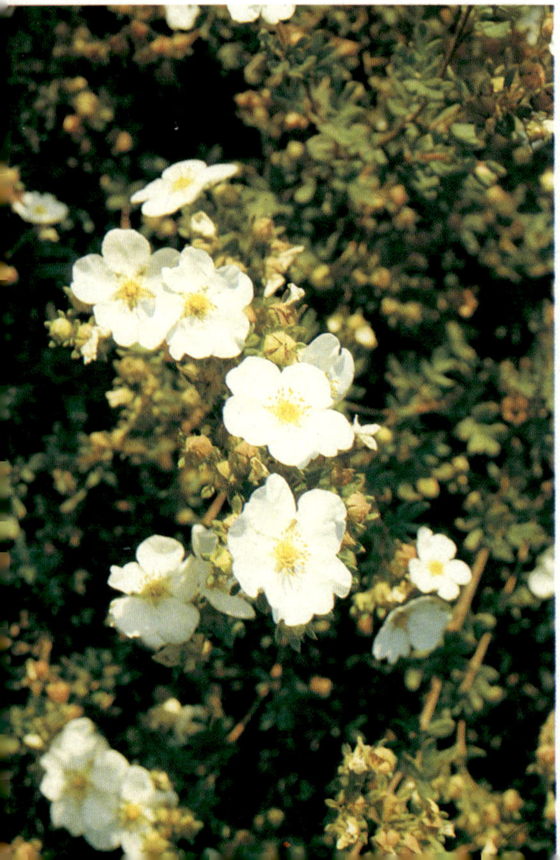
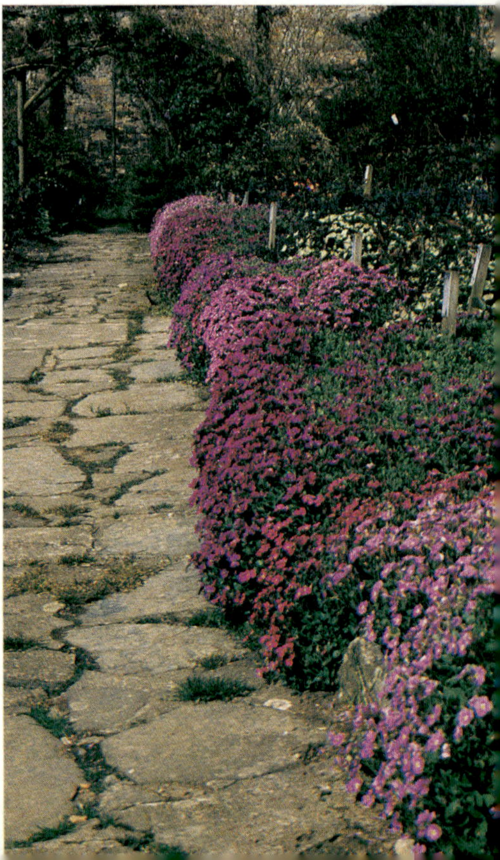

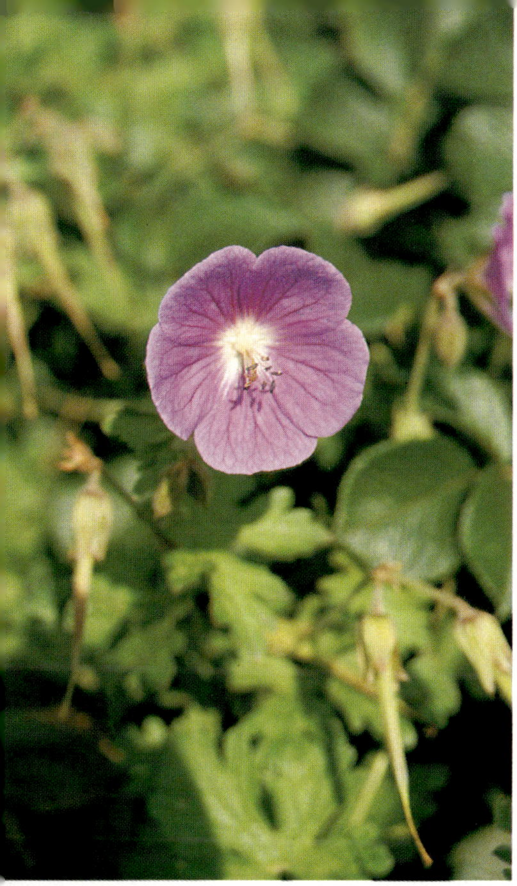
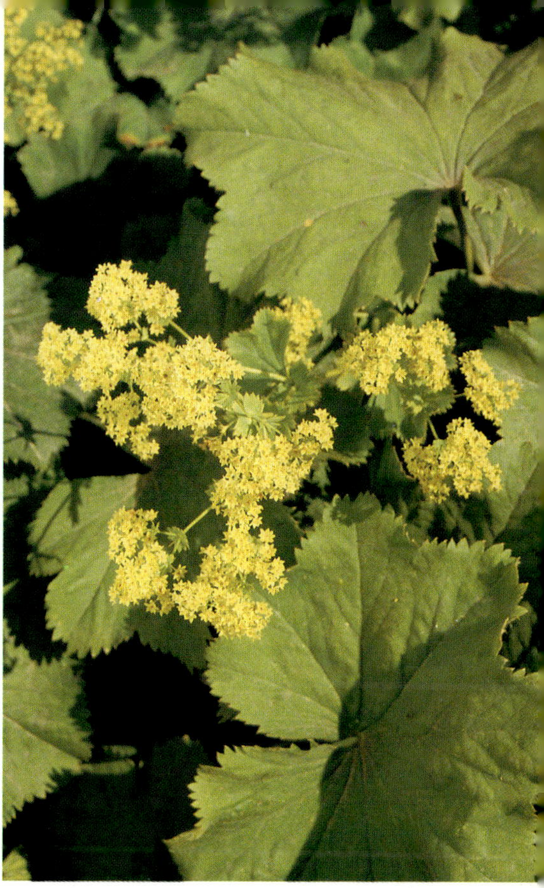
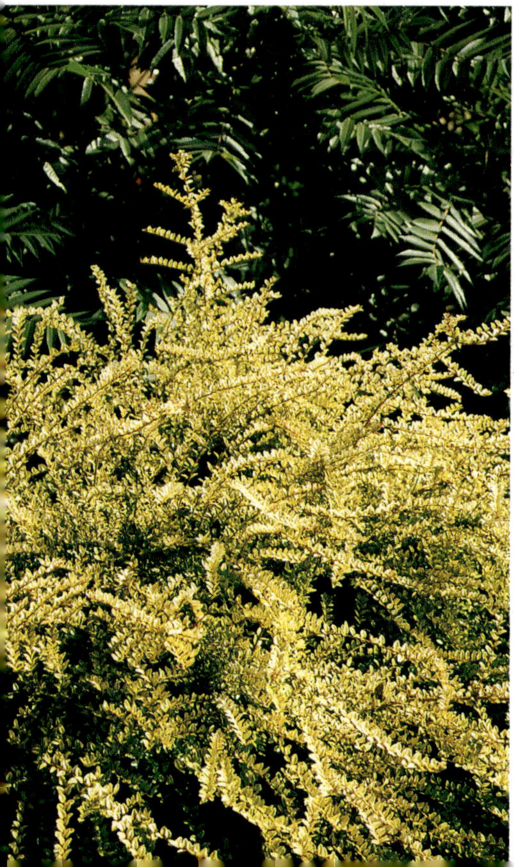
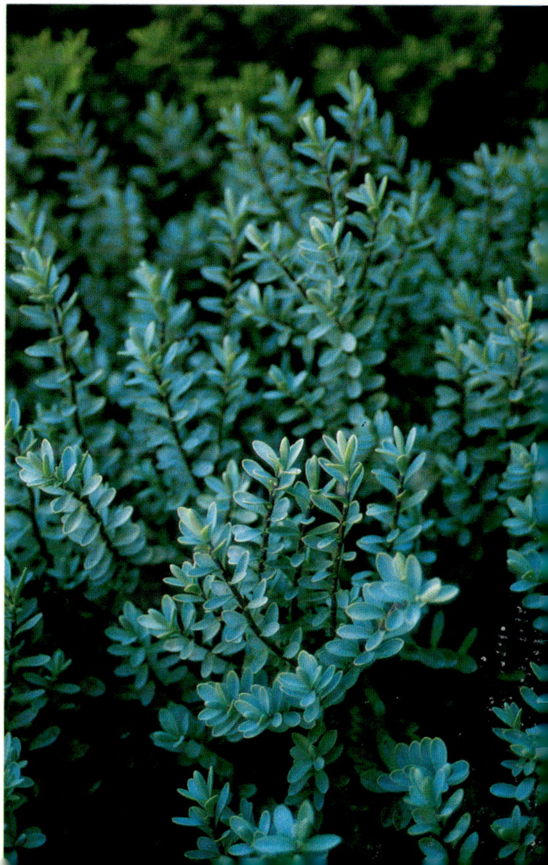

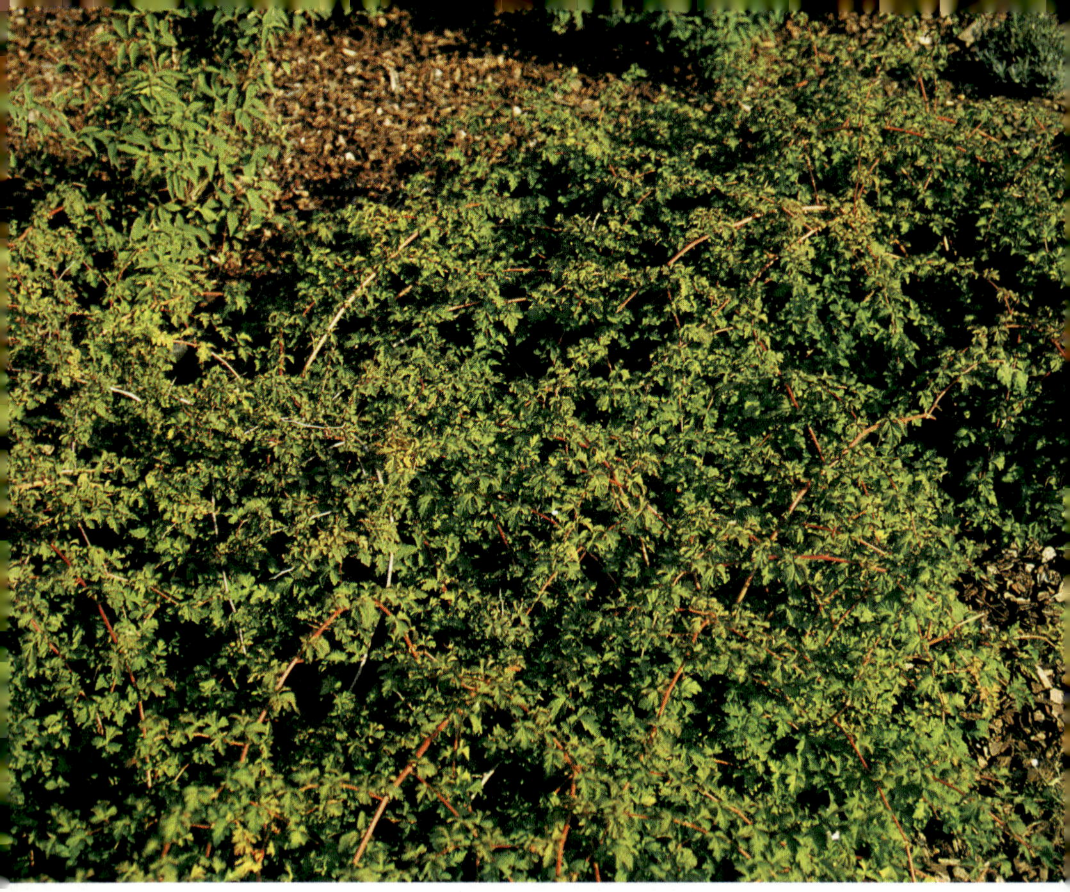

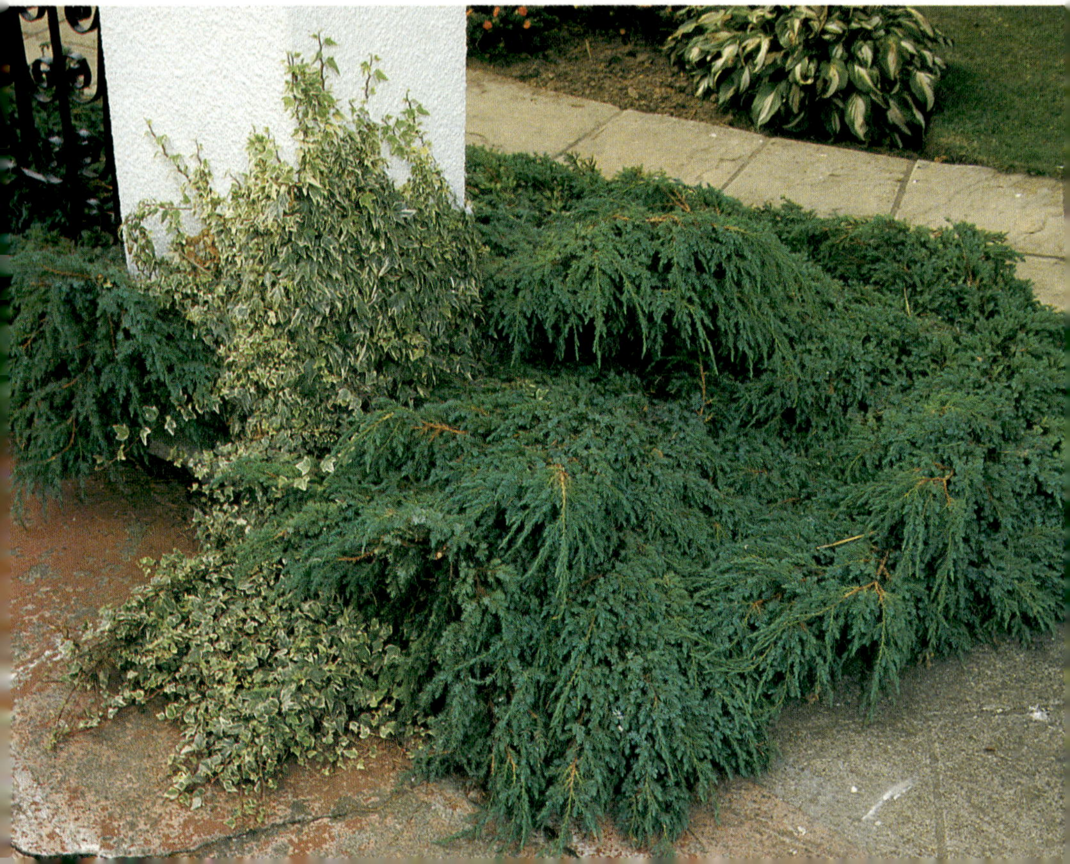

GROUND COVER FOR PARTIALLY SHADED AREAS

Carpet', which is not invasive, but makes good cover, having brightly speckled leaves and yellow flowers in late spring. It grows about 9 inches (20 cm) tall and requires spacing about 12 inches apart. *L. maculatum* is a much stronger grower, with deep pink flowers and marbled leaves. There is a pale pink form, 'Roseum', and two of more disciplined growth: 'Beacon Silver', with striking, silver-white foliage, and 'White Nancy', which has white flowers and silver-grey leaves. No regular attention is necessary, but you may find you get a tidier and better leaf effect if the plants are cut back every year in spring. Spacings for *L. maculatum* and 'Roseum': 15 inches (38 cm) apart; for 'Beacon Silver' and 'White Nancy' 12 inches (30 cm) away from their neighbours.

Most ornamental grasses prefer sunny situations, but **Luzula sylvatica 'Marginata'** will thrive in dry shade. It has broad, deep green leaves and greenish flower heads. Space plants 12 inches (30 cm) apart. When in flower this grass grows to a height of 18 inches (45 cm).

Variegated ginger mint, *Mentha* × *gentalis* 'Variegata', is a very strong mint with leaves attractively variegated green and gold, but it is exceptionally invasive, so needs to be sited carefully. It does have the advantage of retaining its colour, even where there is no sun at all, so is useful for brightening up a dull area. It grows fairly tall – 18 inches (45 cm) before flowering. Space plants at least 15 inches (38 cm) apart.

Another herb with a strong smell and golden leaves which keeps its colour well in shade is the golden form of lemon balm, ***Melissa officinalis* 'Aurea'**. During the winter and early spring it covers the ground where it is rooted with rosettes of yellow leaves, which soon

---

Geranium 'Johnson's Blue' (*top left, previous page*) spreads by suckers

Alchemilla mollis (*top right, previous page*) will spread quickly in sun or partial shade once established

Lonicera 'Baggesen's Gold' as ground cover at the front of a border (*bottom left, previous page*)

Hebe pageii (*bottom right, previous page*) roots where it touches so will help to bind loose earth

Stephanandra 'Crispa' (*above*) – ground cover for an open site

Prostrate forms of juniper (*below*) **are excellent ground cover**

grow up as the weather warms, until shoots up to 2 feet (60 cm) or more are produced, which eventually carry insignificant lilac-blue flowers. The leaves when brushed against or crushed smell strongly of lemon. Space at 15-inch (38-cm) intervals.

If either ginger mint or golden lemon balm becomes too tall and the stems start to flop over, the plants can be cut back to ground level and they will soon grow up again. In any case, it looks better if the whole area is cut back in the autumn.

Polygonatum multiflorum (Solomon's seal) is a well-known 'cottage garden' favourite, with arching sprays up to 2½ feet (80 cm) tall with bell-like flowers along them in early summer. The leaves colour well before the stems die back in autumn. Once settled, the clumps spread briskly. Initial spacing is 15 inches (38 cm) apart.

The **knotgrasses** described on page 45 are just as successful in partial shade as they are in full sun, but some of the taller, more lax forms, such as *Polygonum campanulatum,* will become even less able to support themselves if drawn up by nearby trees, so in such situations it is possibly wiser to choose one of the more compact species, for example, *P. affine.*

The **herbaceous potentillas** will grow and flower well in half-shade, but where the area receives no sun at all, flowering will be affected. For recommended ground cover varieties, see pages 46–47.

Pulmonaria (lungwort or spotted dog) plants are as invaluable for their thick summer coverage of marbled or spotted leaves as they are for their spring flowers. The broad leaves are produced at ground level, and the red, pink, blue or white flowers are produced on stems less than 12 inches (30 cm) tall. There are many good forms, like *P. saccarata argentea* (silvery-white leaves and pink-budded blue flowers); 'Bowles' Red'; 'Marjory Fish' (mottled foliage and pink flowers which does well in dry shade; some of the other varieties can wilt badly if conditions get too dry); and 'Sissinghurst White'. No attention is necessary other than an occasional tidying up of the planting by removing spent flower heads and dead leaves. Space plants 12–15 inches (30–38 cm) apart.

Mossy hybrids of **saxifraga** will grow and flower quite well in partial shade, but in darker places the foliage grows thin and floppy, and few flowers are formed. To be successful, the clumps should receive at least some sunshine, especially in summer. Another 'cottage garden' flower, *Saxifraga urbium* (London Pride) has large rosettes of

GROUND COVER FOR PARTIALLY SHADED AREAS

London Pride

slightly succulent leaves and dainty stems of pink flowers in early summer. It is a highly adaptable plant, as is its very pleasing gold-variegated form. No special care is needed, but the cover looks better with the dead flower heads trimmed off. Space at intervals of 12 inches (60 cm).

Sedum spurium and its coloured and variegated-leaved varieties are similar to the mossy saxifrages in requirements; some shade is no problem but they do not like it too dense. For further details see page 73.

Symphytum grandiflorum 'Variegatum' is a low-growing comfrey with leaves brightly variegated golden yellow, and bluish-white, bell-shaped flowers tinged pink. It spreads quite purposefully, though not as quickly as its all-green counterpart, which is invaluable as ground cover in really difficult places. Plants should be spaced 15 inches (38 cm) apart.

Many forms of the large **viola** family thrive in partial or even total shade. *Viola odorata,* the sweet violet, is famous for its early spring, scented flowers, but it is not as well-known for its excellence as a ground-cover plant as the leaves are comparatively large and it is capable of spreading rapidly (too rapidly, sometimes!) both by its tough, running stems and by seed. *V. cucullata* is also useful, and has several good cultivars, like the blue-flecked 'Freckles'. *V. lutea,* the yellow 'Mountain violet' also blends well with these. There are many other species and cultivars with variously coloured flowers, including a very pretty apricot form. Initial spacing should be 9–12 inches (20–30 cm) apart.

Waldsteinia ternata makes an evergreen carpet of shiny leaves and there are yellow flowers in spring. It will also flourish in full sun. Space plants 12 inches (20 cm) apart. **Heuchera, tierella, tellima** and **heucherella** (see pages 41–49) will also tolerate some shade and the leaf forms are useful for combining with other lower-growing types of herbaceous ground cover. I find *Tellima grandiflora purpurea* mixes extremely well with pulmonaria and *Geranium macrorrhizum* 'Walter Ingwersen', while *Heuchera* 'Palace Purple' blends nicely with some of the more compact varieties of hosta.

Ground cover for heavy shade

A satisfactory ground-cover scheme where the shade is really heavy is much more difficult to achieve. For a start, parts of the garden which are densely shaded often look dreary and need brightening up, and yet you cannot use the sort of plants with very bright flowers and a long season which would do this, because they just would not thrive in such conditions. Also, you could have a problem with soil moisture (too much or too little, according to the kind of shade it is), which makes it necessary to use plants with a high level of tolerance over a wide range of conditions. The snag with some of these is that often they do not look very cheerful. The art of planning a successful ground-cover planting in these circumstances therefore is to contrast colour and foliage form and texture as much as you can so that you end up with something not just functional but interesting as well.

Heavily shaded areas usually fall into two categories: those which are created by tall buildings and similar solid structures excluding all sunshine, and those under mature and very large trees. The former areas tend to be damp; the latter can be very dry, especially when the situation is at its worst – that is, where the trees are evergreen, particularly coniferous. Ground under conifers is virtually impossible to plant up attractively as it is so terribly dry all the year round because of the thick, virtually waterproof canopy formed by the trees; also, the debris – like needles and dead foliage which conifers shed all the year round – contains resins which act as a very efficient and slightly toxic mulch, and this makes it difficult to establish young plants of any sort.

Two plants which you could consider if you have this problem and prefer to see something growing rather than bare earth are an excessively rampant form of dead-nettle and an over-enthusiastic viola – *Viola labradorica*. The dead-nettle which I have seen growing moderately well is *Lamium galebdolon* 'Variegata', which is quite a pretty plant if it were not so rapid-spreading. It is definitely the sort of plant you should treat with the utmost caution, because under better conditions it can fill a garden in a couple of seasons, but in this kind of position it will have its activities severely curtailed until it becomes of quite respectable habit.

L. galebdolon 'Variegata' has prostrate, fast-growing stems which root at intervals into the soil, and pleasant, silver and white leaves which are vaguely nettle-shaped. During early summer it has yellow 'dead-nettle' flowers. The other beauty of this plant, apart from its tenacity, is the fact that once it is securely rooted into the soil it is virtually impossible to get it out without actually digging it up, which means it will stand any amount of raking when you want to have a tidy-up; and when you feel it is becoming too much of a tangle you can shear the whole lot over and it will spring up again from the base. I know someone with a large piece of ground under pine trees which is planted up with this and once a year they cut the entire bed off with a 'strimmer'. Then all they do is rake up both the old stems and the rubbish from the trees and remove it – the area looks wonderfully tidy for a month or two!

Viola labradorica would also be much more attractive as a garden plant if it were not so difficult to snub. It has purple-tinted, violet-like leaves and blue-violet flowers at most times of the year except mid-winter. The young leaves are a highly attractive shade of purple-maroon. As the plant gets older it forms a woody, creeping rootstock which, like the dead-nettle, is very hard to pull out; the base of the plant is usually left in the soil and it will quickly regrow from this. *V. labradorica* reproduces promiscuously, shedding seeds everywhere which all seem to germinate, and there is little that offends the seedlings; I have even seen them growing quite healthily under a thick canopy of hostas, which just goes to show that some plants are impervious to the ground-cover treatment! But although *V. labradorica* can be a nuisance, it also has its uses itself as ground cover where there is really dense shade, and none can be denser or less welcoming to plants than that under evergreens. Again, it can be shorn off once or twice a year if it starts to look untidy, which will help the colour of the massed plants, and it will not be damaged by vigorous cleaning up in the vicinity.

Where the area to be covered is very problematic, it is advisable to plant *Lamium galebdolon* 'Variegatum' about 15 inches (38 cm) apart in order to establish a quick spread, but where conditions are less troublesome it can be spaced much wider apart. I generally plant *Viola labradorica* about 9 inches (20 cm) apart under conifers as the young plants are very small and compact and can soon get lost if you cut down on the quantity. Again, where the site is more encouraging, they can be positioned much further apart.

You will always have some difficulty in keeping the planting tidy where there are large trees causing the shade, as every autumn enormous numbers of dead leaves are deposited on the ground cover underneath. Where shrubs are concerned, it does not matter unduly, except the leaves are prone to stick in the branches and eventually look a bit of a mess; but where lower, herbaceous plants have been used, they can become smothered, which does not do them much good, and also the leaves provide shelter for pests like slugs and snails which will appreciate your on-site catering and can inflict quite a lot of damage, even over winter. Suitable plants must be able to withstand being trampled on, raked over and maybe even cut hard back while still coming up smiling and looking good.

Parts of the garden in deep shade usually look dull, and it is a good idea to use plants with brightly coloured leaves – like the dead-nettle, for example. However, those which retain their colour without any sun at all are limited, and so if you have a large piece of ground to fill, you will possibly have to resort to using green-leaved species as well, but the effect can be improved if they are teamed up with some of the more cheery ones.

If the shade is not caused by big trees, you probably will not have any trouble with moisture in the soil; on the contrary sometimes it can be too much on the damp side. However, all shade under trees, no matter what the variety, is likely to be much drier than normal, so for the year or two following planting, the youngsters must be given every help by not letting the roots dry out, giving a good soaking once or twice a week in summer if necessary, and a mulch of well-rotted compost, farmyard manure, peat, bark, or any other suitable moisture-conserving substance can be applied to the damp soil to keep as much water in as possible. However, it should be remembered that moisture will be lost from the soil not only by evaporation but through the trees' roots absorbing it as well, so even if a mulch has been used, supplementary watering may still have to be given in the early stages.

Shrubs suitable for ground cover in heavy shade

Aucuba japonica (spotted laurel) is a large, leathery-leaved shrub which is capable of surviving just about every nasty it is likely to encounter, including traffic pollution. Left to its own devices it makes quite a tall bush in time, but it can be pruned to more or less any size you require. Male and female flowers are carried on different plants and if the females are pollinated they produce large red berries. Most of the forms in cultivation have some yellow variegation on the leaf which does not seem to be affected by lack of sunshine. The most attractive forms are 'Crotonifolia' which is male, and has heavily speckled leaves; 'Gold Dust', which is similar, but female, 'Picturata', another male form with elongated gold markings, 'Variegata', female, with yellow spots, and 'Salicifolia', an exceptionally free-berrying form with all-green leaves. Space plants 4 feet (1.2 m) apart, or a little less if you want fast coverage.

Ivy makes a wonderful carpeting plant. If it is allowed to run over the ground it produces ordinary roots along the stems instead of aerial ones, and in time it makes an impenetrable mat of evergreen leaves. Most ivies are suitable; even in a dark corner the coloured-leaved sorts keep their variegation well. *Hedera colchica* (Persian ivy) has very large, smooth leaves which are ideal for smothering weeds. The all-green species is attractive in its own right, but it has two very nice and easily obtainable cultivars 'Dentata Aurea', which is brightly variegated yellow, and 'Paddy's Pride', with a central splash of sulphur yellow shading to green. For really rapid coverage, *H. hibernica* (Irish ivy), takes some beating and can be used as flat cover underneath taller plants in a ground-cover scheme.

H. helix (common ivy) has innumerable cultivars with variously shaped and coloured leaves; I find one of the best is 'Glacier' with whitish-grey markings on the leaves and a pink tinge to some of the younger ones in winter. 'Chicago Variegata' is similar, but without the pink. If you are looking for an all-green cultivar, there is 'Cristata' which has crinkled edges to the leaves. I have heard it said that this is not entirely hardy, but have never had any trouble with it personally, and it makes an interestingly textured carpet in the right place. Space plants at intervals of 2½ feet (80 cm) or more, according to the amount of hurry you are in.

Lonicera pileata belongs to the same genus as 'Baggesen's Gold' which I have already described as making good ground cover for an open area (see page 24), but this plant does not mind a dark position and is quite often planted in the countryside under larger bushes and trees as cover for pheasants. It is not a particularly exciting shrub, but it always looks healthy regardless of position, which says a great deal for it. It has a horizontal branch system, with evergreen or semi-evergreen box-like dark green leaves. The plant reaches no more than 2 feet (60 cm) in height but where the branches touch the ground they often root and so the bush can spread quite wide in time – to 4½ feet (1.5 m) or thereabouts. In some seasons blue-purple berries are produced which are attractive to a great many species of birds. Space plants 2½ feet (80 cm) apart for quick results.

Mahonia aquifolium (Oregon grape) is the toughest of all the mahonias, and is a small bush, growing to about 3 feet (1 m) high, with leathery, shiny, pinnate leaves and yellow flowers in spring. It spreads by means of suckering stems and, once established, makes quite thick cover, although it is slow to move in very dry places. It has blue berries in autumn which, like *Lonicera pileata*, will attract birds into the garden. Space plants at intervals of 2½ feet (80 cm).

Prunus laurocerasus **'Otto Luyken'**, **'Schipkaensis'** and **Zabeliana'** are three forms of cherry laurel with a low, spreading, dense growth habit and narrow, shiny evergreen leaves. In early summer, and sometimes again in the autumn, they have upright racemes of white flowers, followed by poisonous, black fruits like small cherries. Plant cherry laurels 3 feet (1 m) apart.

Rubus tricolor is an ornamental bramble which fairly gallops once established. It has a prostrate, rambling habit; the stems root into the soil at intervals at the tips to form new plants. They are red and covered with soft prickles. The leaves are glossy with white felt underneath. The small, purple flowers are inconspicuous and sometimes develop into edible red fruits. ***R. tricolor*** will stand dry conditions providing the soil is not dust-dry. Initial spacing is 2½–3 feet (80 cm-1 m) apart.

Ruscus aculeatus (butcher's broom), a curious small evergreen shrub, has evergreen, spine-tipped 'cladodes' ('apparent' leaves) and green, stiff stems. Male and female flowers are on separate plants and if the female flowers are pollinated they will produce red berries. The plants spread slowly by suckering; in some parts of Britain they grow wild at the edge of mixed woods. This is another subject which will encourage birds and other small wildlife. Ruscus should be spaced about 2½ feet (80 cm) apart.

Sarcococca is a genus of small, evergreen shrubs with

Matteuccia struthiopteris

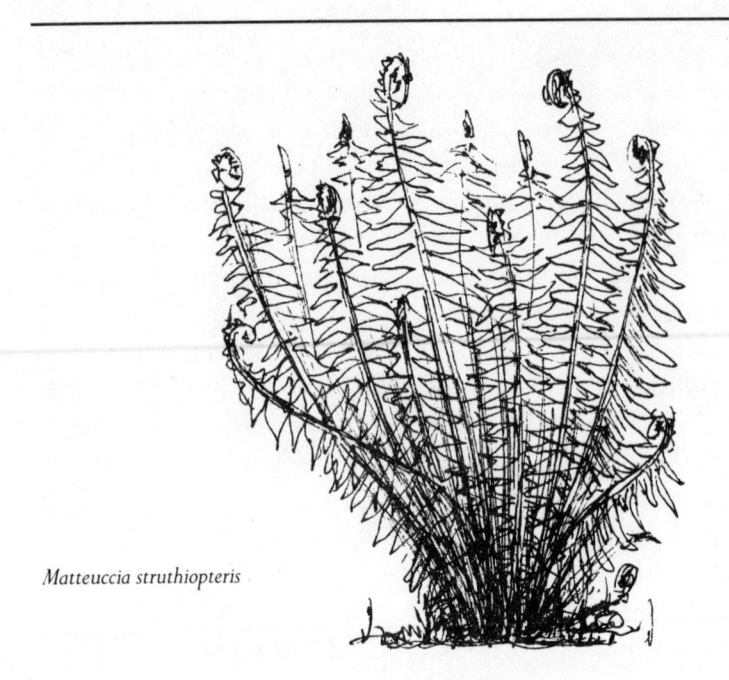

white flowers which have a strong and sweet scent in late winter, followed by black berries. Those usually to be found in garden centres include *S. hookerana dignya*, the largest in the group, which reaches about 6 feet (2 m) in height and spreads by suckers; *S. humilis,* a much smaller, thicket-forming shrub, and *S. ruscifolia,* a slow-growing shrub about 2½ feet (80 cm) tall. Spacing for *S. dignya* is 3–4 feet (1–1.2 m) apart; for *S. humilis* 2 ½ feet (80 cm); and for *S. ruscifolia* 2 feet (60 cm) apart. Occasionally one comes across two other very small forms – *S. confusa* and *S. chinensis,* which is a faster grower. Spacing for these is the same as for *S. humilis* and *S. ruscifolia* respectively.

Herbaceous plants for heavy shade
Apart from *Lamium galebdolon* 'Variegatum' and *Viola labradorica,* there are very few herbaceous perennials which thrive in dense shade that are useful as ground cover. Periwinkle (vinca) which is sometimes thought of as a herbaceous perennial and sometimes as a dwarf shrub is perhaps the most successful. The greater periwinkle, *Vinca major,* is not a particularly tidy or exciting-looking plant, having long, straggly, trailing stems which, like *Rubus tricolor,* root at the ends and then set off all over again, but it has pretty blue flowers in early summer and

looks considerably better if, once the desired density has been reached, it is trimmed back to the base in spring and again sometime during the summer. Its variegated counterpart is identical in all respects except that the leaves are splashed with cream, but it is much more pleasing as a ground-cover subject and seems to retain its variegation even in quite dark situations. The lesser periwinkle, *V. minor,* and its variously coloured flowered and variegated cultivars are not so tough and strong-growing, so are more suited to areas which have a little more sunshine, but I have seen a good cover using the plum-coloured flowered form, *V. minor* 'Atropopurea'. Space plants at intervals of 1½–2 feet (45–60 cm).

The only other herbaceous perennial which as far as I am concerned is worth trying is a dwarf comfrey, **Symphytum grandiflorum**. This grows to little more than 9 inches (20 cm) in height, with leaves which are rather foxglove-shaped, only rougher, and creamy-white flowers in spring. It spreads rapidly and will soon smother any intruders, but as far as looks are concerned, it doesn't set the world alight, although combined with, say *Viola labradorica* and the two allowed to intermingle it looks better than bare earth, if not much! The variegated form seems to need some sun to produce its best yellow variegations. Spacing 15 inches (38 cm).

In constantly moist ground **Matteuccia struthiopteris,** the ostrich feather fern, can be used as ground cover. Cost should not be the first consideration, however, as it has an upright habit and therefore needs close planting at intervals of 18 inches (45 cm).

Ground cover to bind loose earth

The most usually occurring instance of loose earth is where land has been excavated, or piled up, forming banks. One way this situation can be dealt with is by constructing a retaining wall for all or part of the slope of the bank; another method is to cover it with concrete slabs. The former idea is not always practicable – for example, where banks have been constructed to screen a bad view or absorb noise – and unless you are handy as a bricklayer or stonemason or have a lot of spare bricks or stone lying about, the exercise could be a very costly one. Concrete slabs do not look particularly attractive although the appearance of the job can be improved quite a lot if you leave sections of earth uncovered and plant something into them – maybe a single specimen or small group of some of the ground-cover plants already described in this book. If you are not agile, or you think you might find scrambling up and down the bank for routine maintenance difficult, then this solution might not be the most practical; if, on the other hand, there is no physical argument against it, then often the best way of dealing with a bank to prevent the soil slipping down to the bottom is to plant something on it.

Of course, you can always use grass. The roots quickly form a dense, binding mat, and nothing looks nicer than slopes of well-cared-for grass. Banks treated in this way are not always easy to care for, however. It is difficult – often impossible – to mow them with an ordinary cylinder mower, unless the slope is very gentle, when it is unlikely you will have a problem with soil erosion anyway. It can even be quite dangerous to cut grass on a steep bank with a mechanically driven mower, even a rotary one with a rope tied to the handle, as there is a risk of stones flying up in your face and a chance you might slip and get tangled up with the machine. And if for some reason you should be unable to look after the bank for a while, it will get very untidy and even more difficult to put to rights.

Clearly, then, the best all-round answer is to use ground-cover plants to cut down eventual maintenance and stop soil slipping downwards. At this point, many readers will think: "Why not turn the whole thing into a large and potentially spectacular rockery?" Well, if you are a dedicated gardener and are prepared to spend a great deal of time weeding and generally tending the alpines, and providing it is possible to adapt the bank as a rockery by implanting large stones which will not only improve the appearance but will retain the soil at various levels, then there is nothing wrong with considering the rockery approach. If, on the other hand, you just want something which will both act as a weed suppressant and a soil binder, which is, once established, relatively self-maintaining and which looks good throughout the year, then ground-cover planting is a must.

To be successful under such conditions, the subjects must be able to retain the soil quickly and efficiently, either by a rapid suckering habit or by the horizontal branches themselves producing roots where they touch the soil. They must also be tolerant of a wide range of soil and moisture conditions.

The top of the bank will, naturally, be the driest area, gradually becoming damper as the slope descends. If you are intending to use the same species at the top of the bank as at the bottom, the plants will have to put up with varying light levels, especially if the banks form the sides of a cutting, as often happens at the side of drives where what might otherwise have been a difficult gradient has been levelled off for the convenience of the motorist or pedestrian. The ideal bank cover plant will also require the minimum of attention, as banks are not the easiest things to negotiate. In addition, it should also give coverage all the year around, preventing weed seeds from germinating and establishing themselves when the cover is less dense at the start and end of the season, as is the case with many herbaceous and deciduous ground-cover subjects.

The kind of plants you are looking for, therefore, are those with underground suckering stems, rapidly spreading, tenacious root systems, or lax stems which run quickly across the ground, rooting where they touch or forming new plants at the ends when in contact with the soil. They should ideally be shrubby or sub-shrubby in characteristics, and evergreen or semi-evergreen. The choice is clearly rather restricted, but this is not to say that simple and effective schemes cannot be devised, as there are an adequate number of plants

THE BIG COVER-UP

to choose from, and if the groups are combined together thoughtfully, blending and shading the various leaf colours and textures, then you should be quite satisfied with the results.

Before going on to describe the plants which fit the bill, we should perhaps look at the construction of the bank itself. It does not matter whether it is up in the air, as in the case of the barrier bank, or in a cutting, the sides should have a reasonable slope to them. This is easy enough to achieve when earth is being moved to construct a barrier, as the sides can be graded, and the degree of slope should preferably be no more than 45° – less if possible – to prevent rain washing the soil down before you have chance to do anything with it. Also, the gentler the degree of slope, the less likely the banks are to crumble away under the weight of the soil at the back of them.

Problems often arise with banks in cuttings, where the drive or path has been taken through, leaving the ground at each side considerably steeper than the recommended angle. This makes the banks especially unstable as the earth at either side will tend to press outwards during times of heavy rainfall or hard frost, and it is not uncommon for the sides to fall away into the newly-formed bottom of the cutting. It is important, therefore, that great attention be given to the gradient of the banks at the time the cutting is made, and if they are going to end up sloping too steeply, then more earth must be taken out until they are less precipitous; this, of course, will also make subsequent cultivation easier.

Banks frequently have a further drawback in that they may have a coverage of little or no topsoil. While the plants I am about to suggest are not fastidious about growing conditions, they will not thrive where topsoil is completely absent or very thin; even if you get them off to a good start by using well-grown containerized specimens in large pots, they will eventually need a root-run wider than the limit of the compost in their pots and when they hit the hard, impoverished sub-soil, their growth will go into a rapid decline. You have to make sure that the banks receive a good covering of decent soil when they are formed – not a very easy job to do, and this is all the more reason why the slope should be as gentle as possible, as it facilitates the spreading of the topsoil. If you are lucky enough to have a natural slope or bank, on the other hand, you should have enough topsoil cover not to present too many problems when you begin to plant up.

GROUND COVER TO BIND LOOSE EARTH

Another time you are likely to meet a sloping piece of ground which is a candidate for bank planting is where the garden changes level markedly in one direction or another. If it is new to you, and you are considering starting from scratch or drastically reorganizing things, there are three courses open to you. The first is to regrade the whole area, creating a long, continual, gentle gradient, which is easy to tend, either as lawn or flower beds, if a little uninspired. The second is to divide the garden into flat areas and terraces retained by walls with steps from one level to the next. This looks very good if done and planted correctly, but can be very costly: even if you do the labour yourself, the price of the right brick or stone can be astronomical.

The third method is somewhat similar to the second, but easier and less expensive, and consists of grading the garden into a series of flat or very gentle slopes, losing the rest of the difference in levels in a steeper bank or banks, which are then planted up with ground-cover plants. If the larger, flatter pieces are then grassed, the design, once put into practice and allowed to mature, is very labour-saving, regular work being confined to mowing the lawn and tending any flower borders you may have created at the sides of the level or nearly level parts. If the gradient of the steeper banks is not excessive, it is much cheaper and more simple as far as mowing is concerned if the more level areas are connected through the bank cover planting with grass paths, then the mower can be run from one part of the garden to the others without any lifting or hauling up and down steps.

Once you are satisfied with the slope and soil of your bank, you may feel your problems to be over, but with newly disturbed soil you may find that, even when you have done everything right, you still get a certain amount of soil movement for the first few years, especially at the beginning, as the loose soil works itself down or is washed to the bottom when it rains heavily. Usually the amount is not great, certainly not enough to cause you to wonder about the stability of the bank, and if there is only grass or an informal path at the base you may decide that the trouble is not serious enough to be worth doing anything about. Where it can become a nuisance, though, is when the slopes run onto a drive, as it can make the sides look permanently untidy and involve more sweeping than should be necessary with what is, after all, supposed to be a low-maintenance scheme. You may feel in these circumstances that it is justifiable to provide a low

THE BIG COVER-UP

retaining wall at the base, a foot or so high, of stone, brick, concrete blocks or even timber, which will soon be hidden as the ground-cover plants grow over it, but will effectively trap all the loose earth as it shuffles down.

A further reason why the type of plants you should use in this kind of situation has to be a bit special is that, unlike almost every other occasion when you are planting new things, you cannot dig the soil thoroughly first, as it will cause even more instability. Providing that the earth for the first foot or so is in reasonable condition, this is the one occasion where I do not recommend digging too large a hole – merely one big enough to take the root system comfortably and enable you to work soil around it thoroughly so that no empty pockets are left. Once you have finished planting, especially if the slope is a long one, it will no doubt look as though a herd of elephants has trampled all over it and the temptation will be to fork all the bits between the plants to improve the appearance of the surface. Unless you know your bank is very solid, however, you should resist the temptation to do this, as it will only make more of the soil loose. Instead, you can give it a very gentle raking or a smoothing with a small hand fork.

For the first summer or so after planting up, you will nearly always encounter a period when the bank becomes very dry, especially if it faces south or west. You will have to provide some artificial watering, particularly at the top, but here again you could have a problem with erosion, and so all water should be applied very carefully in the form of a mist, which can generally be obtained through the hand-held nozzle produced as a hose-end attachment by some of the better manufacturers (see page 142). Another of the attachments allows for the insertion of a fertilizer tablet, thus enabling you to water and apply liquid feed at the same time.

Where bank plantings are undertaken on a very large scale, for example on urban ring-roads and in municipal landscaping schemes, much use is made of chipped and pulverized bark. This has the double benefit of reducing weeds and conserving soil moisture, but if

---

The variegated form of *Cotoneaster horizontalis* – a versatile ground cover shrub

Euphorbia amygdaloides 'Rubra' – ideal cover for partial shade

Leaf detail (*overleaf, above*) of *Tellima grandiflora* 'Purpurea' – a herbaceous cover plant for partial shade

Hydrangeas used as ground cover (*overleaf, below*)

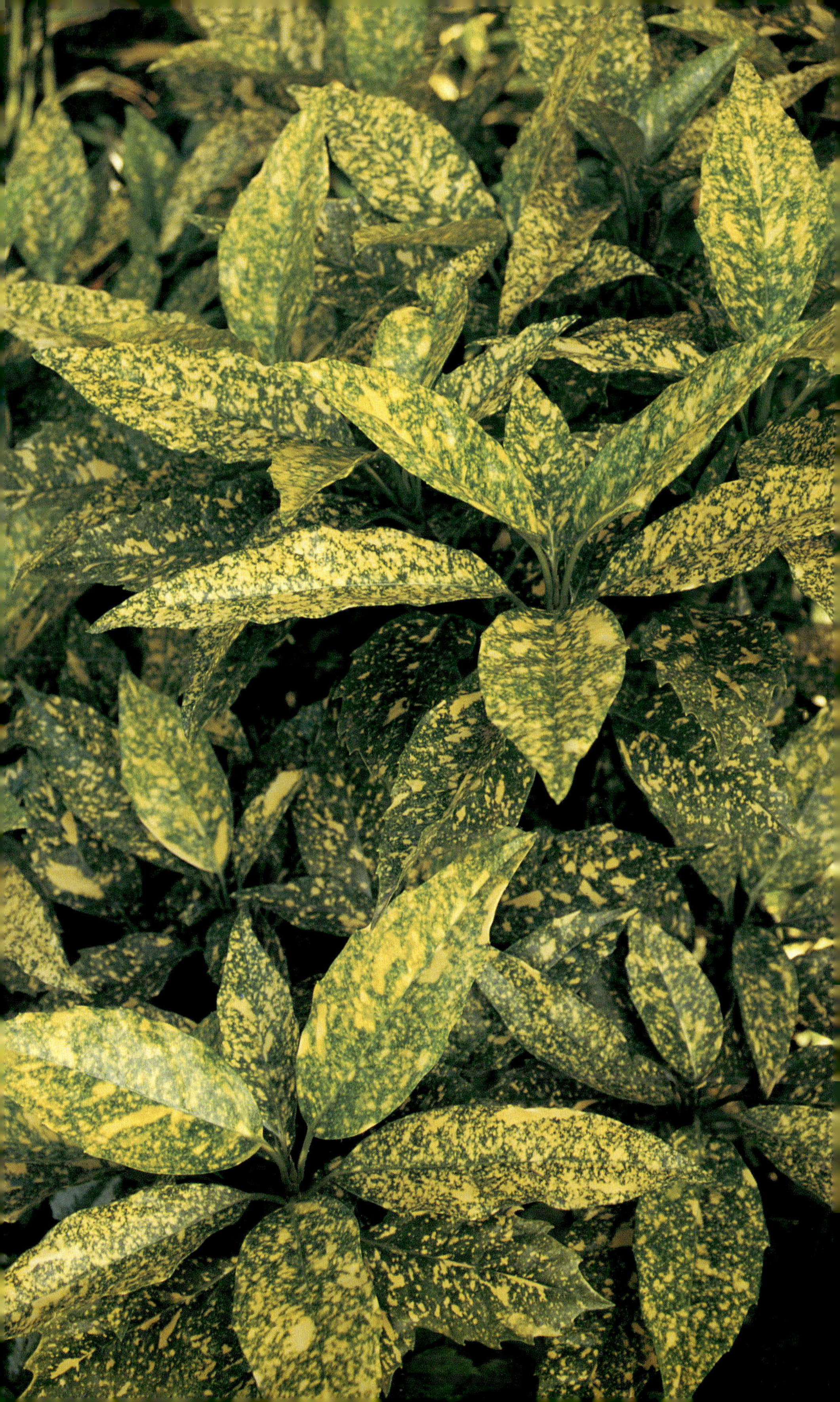

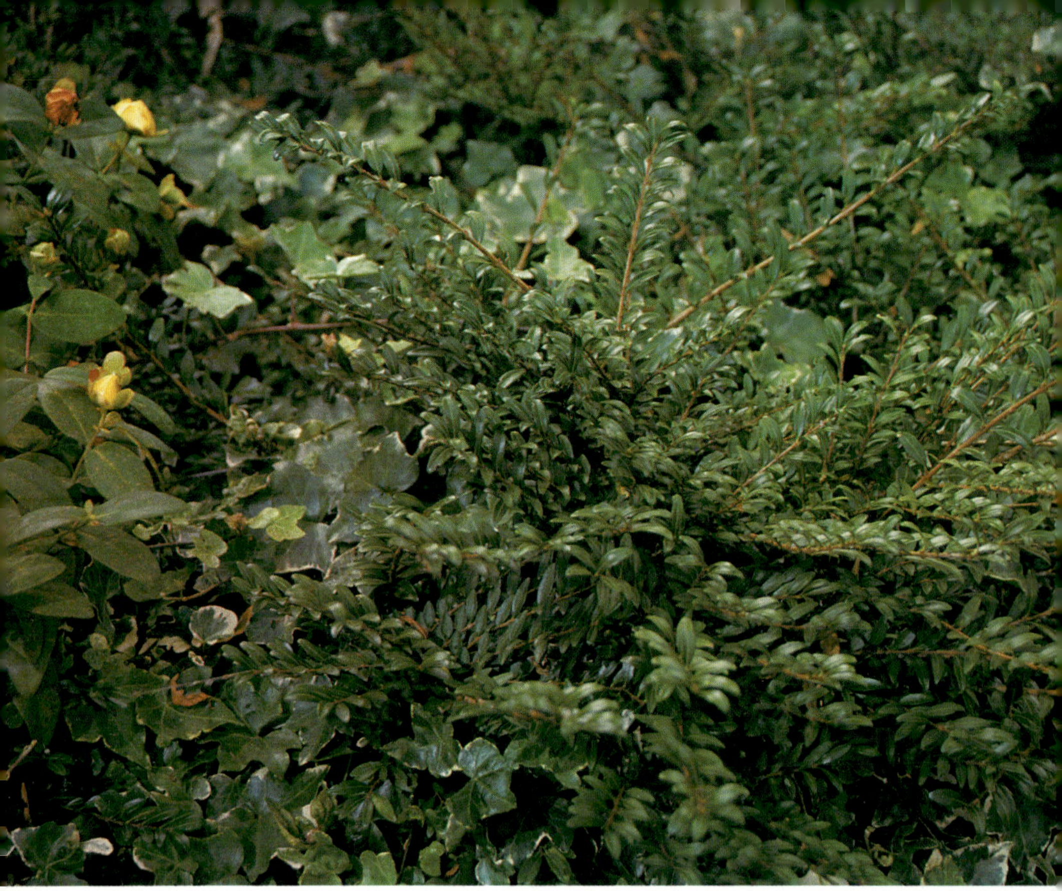

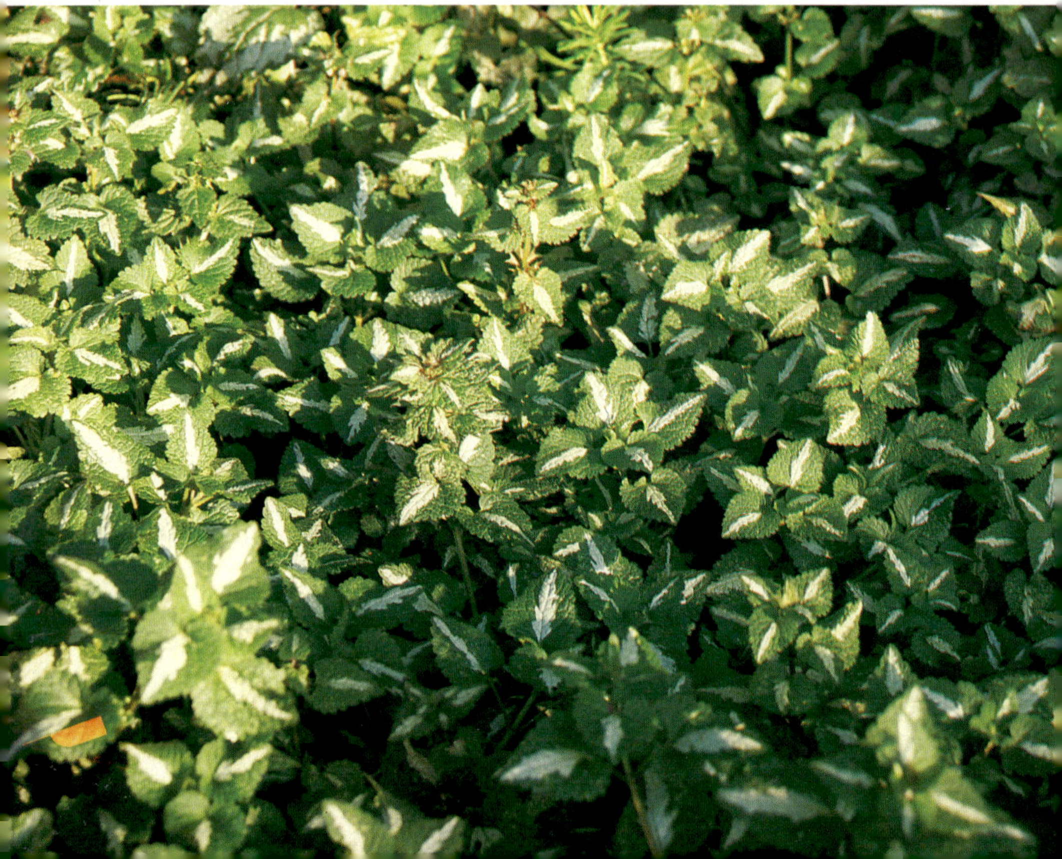

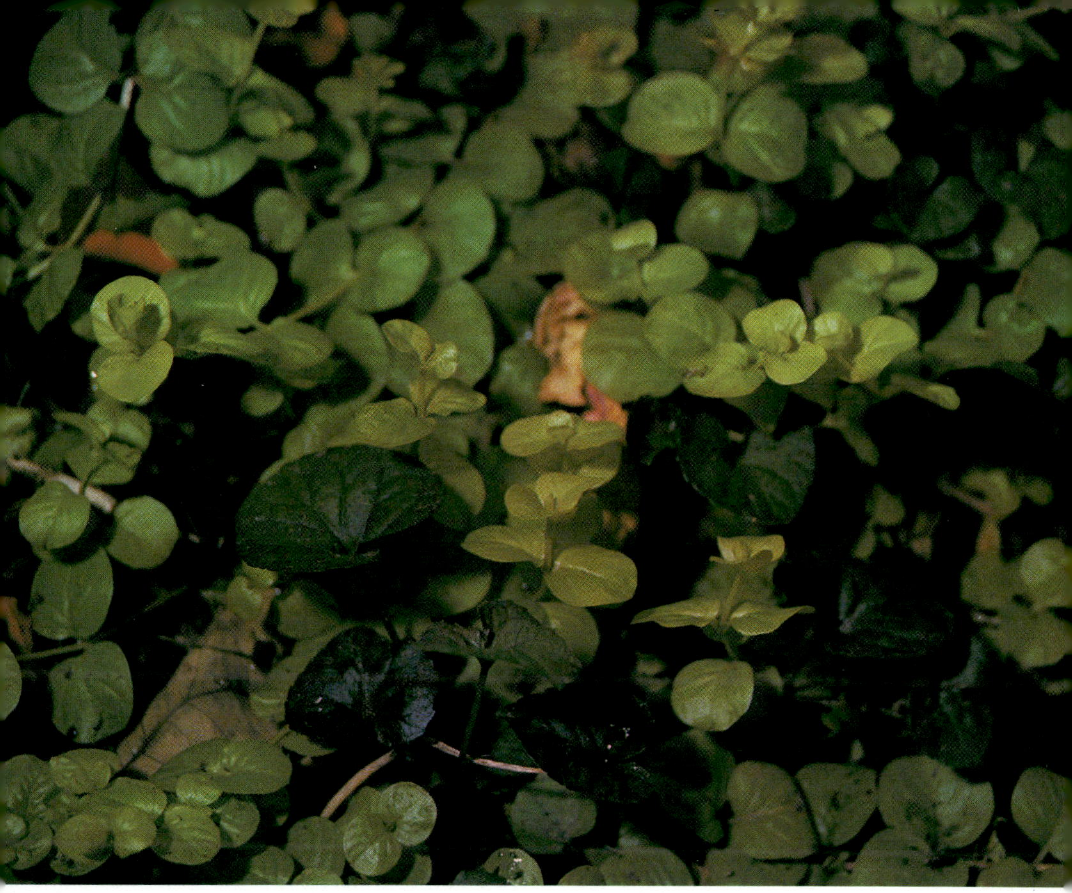

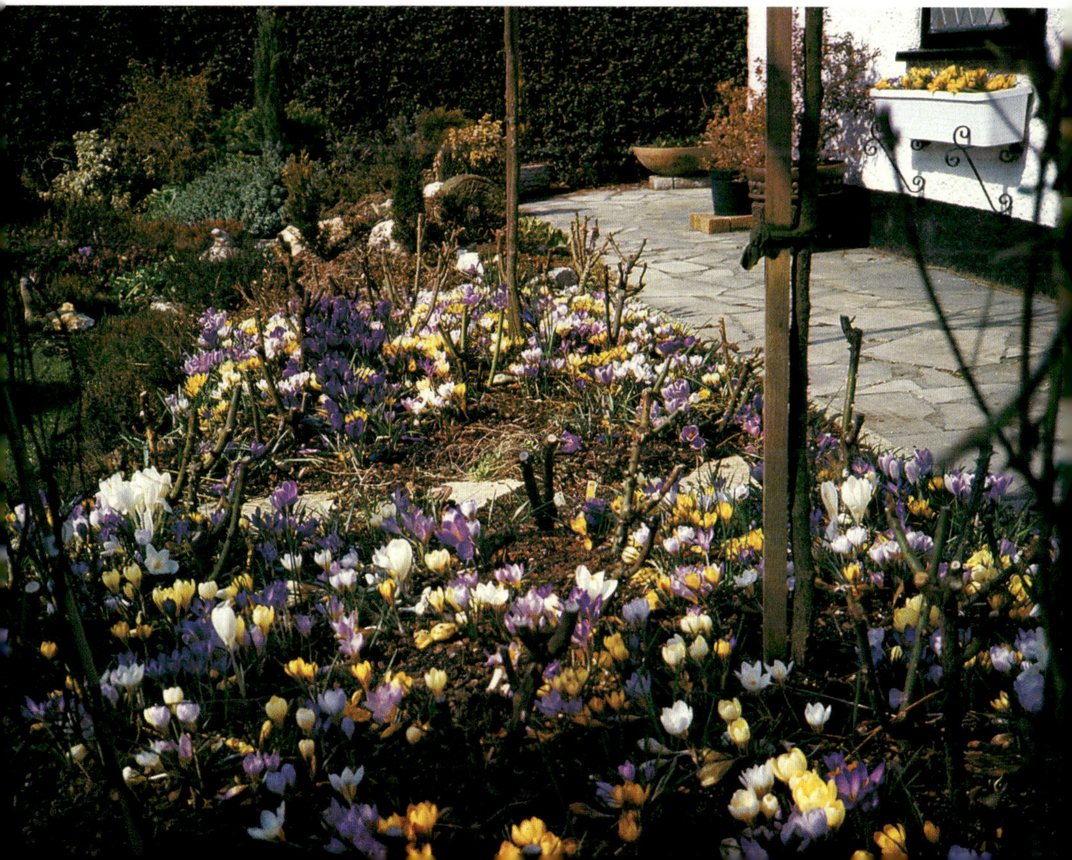

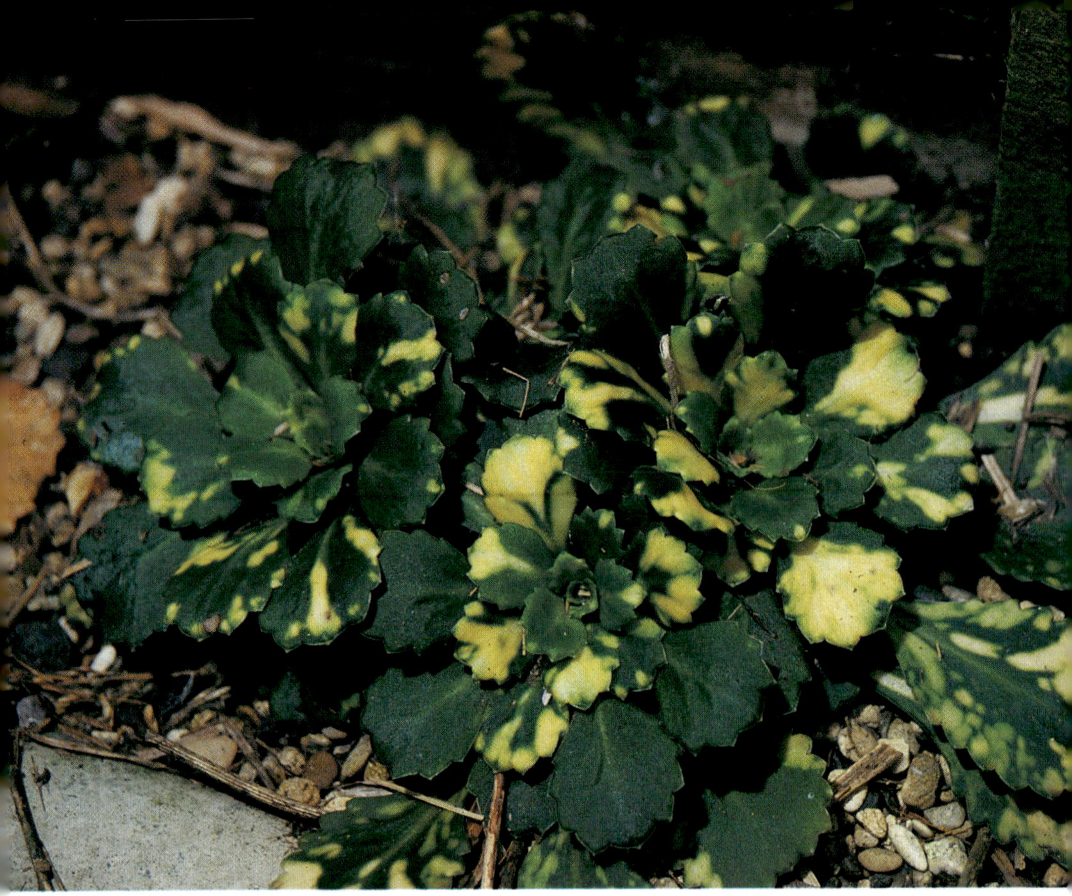

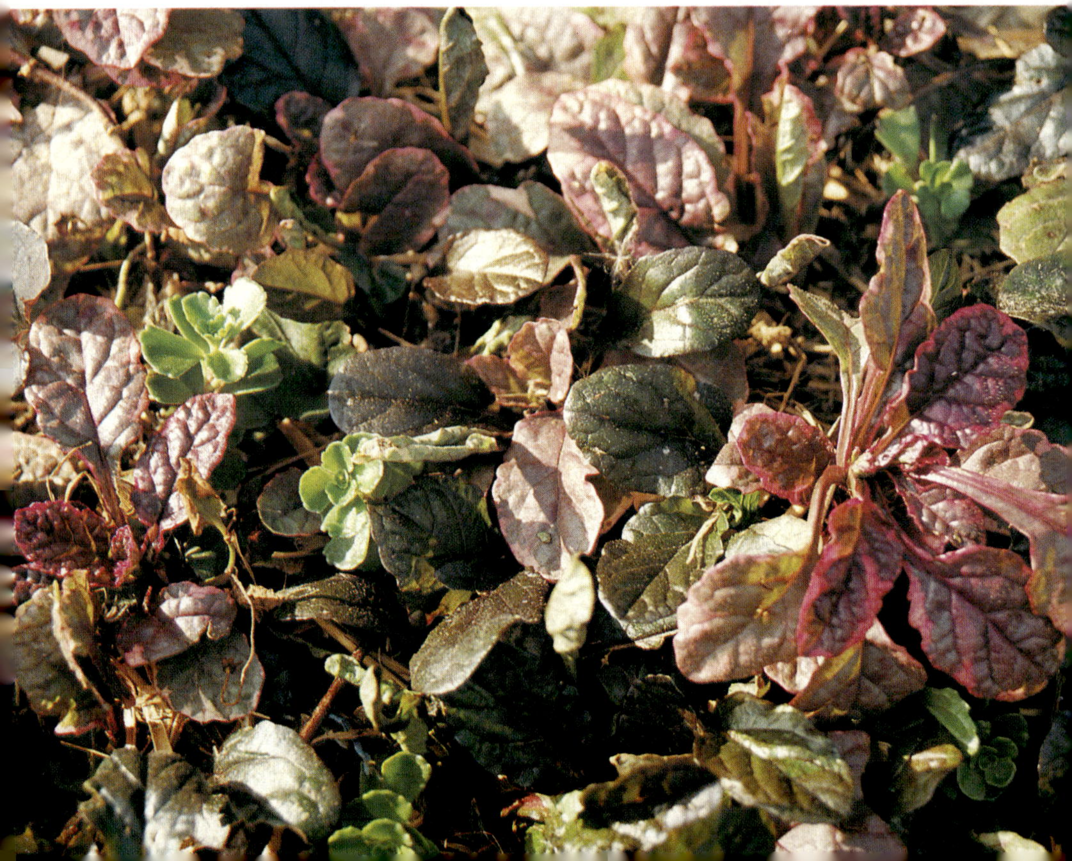

you are considering using this form of mulch, it may be advisable to read the cautionary comments on page 9 first, especially if you like a tidy garden.

Of course, you are likely to have a problem with weeds until total coverage is attained. It is unwise to hoe, as you really need the surface of the soil to remain as undisturbed as possible, so the only other non-chemical answer is hand-weeding, which may or may not be practical according to circumstances. The only other answer is to resort to a total weedkiller temporarily; I find the best as far as ease of application and length of effect is concerned is 'Casoron G4' applied in late February. Used according to manufacturer's instructions, it should have no effect on the majority of the subjects listed in this chapter, but where it *is* unwise to use it this is mentioned. However, if you are thinking of brightening up the scheme by underplanting with spring bulbs, it is inadvisable to use Casoron G4 as some damage is likely to occur.

The plants listed here as being suitable for binding earth are the ones which in my work as a landscape gardener I find most successful; however, most plants in this book will hold a bank together in time as nearly all of them have root systems which are good for that purpose. Many species can be experimented with and will usually be successful, though the spacings may need closing up to ensure rapid coverage.

Shrubs and herbaceous plants

It should be stressed that, where the soil is strongly alkaline, **Cornus canadensis** (creeping dogwood – see page 19) will not be happy and so should only be used on banks with a pH of less than 6.5. This plant will quickly bind earth with its creeping underground stems. Many birds enjoy the red berries in autumn. It is not evergreen but the mass of low, deciduous stems is usually enough to deter all but the most adventurous weeds. Along with many other plants which prefer more acid conditions, *C. canadensis* may show signs of chlorosis if Casoron G4 is used as a pre-emergent weedkiller and so mulching is more advisable as a weed suppressant.

A variegated form of spotted laurel – a shrub that will tolerate quite heavy shade (*previous page*)

Lonicera pileata (*above*) can be used as ground cover in conditions of dense shade

Lamium maculatum (*below*) – a dead nettle that will spread in shade

THE BIG COVER-UP

All low-growing and prostrate forms of **cotoneaster** are excellent for bank planting, but the ones like *Cotoneaster dammeri* (humifusus) and 'Coral Beauty' are more satisfactory than *C. horizontalis*, *C. conspicuus decorus* and *C. microphyllus* as they are very good at producing roots along their stems, whereas the other forms are more effective at preventing erosion by protecting the surface of the soil from attack by wind, sun, rain and frost. See pages 19–20 for a description of varieties and recommended spacing distances.

***Euonymus radicans* 'Variegata'** (*E. fortunei* 'Silver Queen') is perhaps the best of the low-growing, evergreen euonymus species as it is fairly quick-growing and the stems readily root where they come in contact with the ground. The clumps themselves also increase in girth and the mass of fibrous roots very effectively keep loose soil in position. It will stand a certain amount of drought once established and requires little attention where access is difficult.

Most other low-growing euonymus (see page 21) will also bind soil, though you may not get as quick results.

Again, ***Epimedium perraldianum*** is probably the best of many epimediums as far as containing soil goes. Its mat-forming habit produced by its creeping stem system and close, fibrous root systems are ideal even though it is not a shrub, but a herbaceous perennial, and it is not entirely evergreen. Its leaves die brownish-orange and leathery and provide good cover, even in winter. See page 63 for spacing distances. As it is a herbaceous perennial, *E. perraldianum* will be adversely affected by the use of weedkillers such as 'Casoron G4', which is only suitable for plants with woody stems, and if you use a mulch of bark chippings thick enough to deter weeds it will tend to deter the spread of the epimedium as well. If you want to tidy the bank up in spring, and provided the slope is not too great, the tops can be mown off with a rotary mower, or where this would be difficult, a 'strimmer' with a nylon line will knock the old growth off.

All low-growing forms of **hebe** are evergreen and even the larger bushes, like *Hebe buxifolia* and *H. anomala*, will root where any of the older stems flop over and touch the soil. However, for efficiency you cannot beat the carpeting forms like *H.* 'Carl Teschner', 'Quicksilver', 'Wingletye' and *H. pinguifolia* 'Pagei'. These root all over the place, never get untidy, will stand hot sun and dry roots and do not need any maintenance if you do not feel like giving them any. Descriptions and spacings are to be found on pages 22–24.

GROUND COVER TO BIND LOOSE EARTH

I was not sure whether to include **variegated ground elder** (see page 64) or not, as I have my reservations of its suitability as a bank plant (it is not shrubby and it is not evergreen), but its mass of underground stems running everywhere make any weeds difficult to establish, while it does do a first-rate job of binding soil. It can look dull in the winter when nearly all the top growth has died off, but I suppose if the site is not really special it could be considered. Spacing distances are given on page 64. Casoron G4 will have a detrimental effect on it, though one application is not likely to annihilate it completely.

Hypericum calycinum (rose of Sharon) is perhaps the most widely planted hypericum species available today, and one which has a bad reputation, though undeservedly so, owing to the fact that on seeing it for the first time, many people fall in love with the very large, yellow flowers, the centres of which are full of red-tipped stamens,

Hypericum calycinum

THE BIG COVER-UP

only to find that it spreads much further than they would have liked. It is a short-growing plant, reaching around 12 inches (30 cm) in height, and increases by suckering stems until it covers a vast area, which is when most gardeners become bored with it. Used in the right place, where there is a lot of space and when you want a dense and binding cover, nothing looks prettier when in full flower, as it can turn an open space or boring bank into a blaze of yellow during summer.

H. calycinum is evergreen, though in the hard winter of 1986–7 our neighbours' planting was severely cut back, though it soon recovered from the base. The appearance of a mass planting is considerably improved if it is trimmed back to the base in spring, where the new growth can already be found. Unfortunately, in recent years it has become very much a martyr to rust disease, which is not only unsightly but can severely affect the strength of the plants. This can be controlled to a certain extent by spraying with 'Tumbleblite'. Space plants 12 inches (30 cm) apart for bank cover; you can position the plants further apart on ordinary, flat ground.

All **ivies** will bind loose soil well, and the varieties to choose really depend on personal preference. Large slopes can look somewhat sombre if dark, plain-leaved forms of ivy are used, so it might be advisable to use those with brightly coloured variegations, such as *Hedera colchica* 'Dentata Aurea' (yellow and green); 'Paddy's Pride', (sulphur yellow centre shading to green); *H. helix* 'Adam' (small leaves margined with white); 'Buttercup' (bright yellow turning yellowish-green); 'Chicago Variegata' (green leaves with purple blotches and a white margin); 'Glacier' (silver-grey, margined white); 'Gold Child' (yellow margins); 'Goldheart' (green with a central splash of gold); 'Marginata Elegantissima' (similar to 'Glacier'); and 'Marmorata Minor' (small leaves mottled cream and grey). See page 78 for information on spacing.

I have included **Lamium galebdolon 'Variegata'** (see page 75) here because it is one of the most rapid soil-binding plants I know, even in really difficult conditions, and the silvery-grey and green effect is attractive, even though using this plant will not give you the tidiest effect. Like epimedium, it can be trimmed off in the spring, and at any other time, if you feel like it, with a hover mower or strimmer when it begins to get out of control.

Mahonia aquifolium (Oregon grape – see page 79) also produces

GROUND COVER TO BIND LOOSE EARTH

suckering stems, but it is rather more civilized of growth habit. It is one of the few slightly taller shrubs suitable for binding soil and can therefore be used for very large areas without looking out of place.

Pachysandra terminalis and *P. t.* 'Variegata' spread by suckering underground stems as well, though they are much smaller in stature. They are better in positions which are not too hot and sunny, and are therefore useful for north-facing banks and slopes. See page 55 for details on spacing and cultivation.

Vincas (periwinkles) produce new plants at the ends of their stems where they touch the soil, so an area of loose earth is soon colonized and consolidated. Most species are suitable (see pages 57 – 59); the more strong-growing forms like *Vinca major* and *V. m.* 'Variegata' give perhaps the best colour as they have larger leaves, but the various forms of *V. minor* should not be discounted, especially for smaller areas. **Rubus tricolor** (see page 79) has a similar habit, although much more rampant, and will cover up a bank where many other plants might have a struggle.

Ground cover in rose beds

There are certain gardening topics which are guaranteed to promote heated discussion, not to say ferocious argument, and the emotive subject of whether or not to use ground cover under otherwise formal plantings of bush roses is one. Those who consider underplanting roses are generally people like myself who both want to maximize every square foot of soil and have gardens with limited space where each plant has to do the job of three as far as aesthetic value is concerned, and what available room there is must not under any circumstances be wasted. Gardeners who are strongly against growing anything in a rose bed other than roses argue that anything else detracts from the beauty of the roses, and the style of the bushes themselves does not lend itself to mixed planting of any sort.

This may be so, but I have seen some very attractive cottage gardens where all types and styles are thrown together, albeit in a 'planned' sort of chaos, bush hybrid tea and floribunda roses hob-nobbing with hardy and half-hardy annuals, perennials, herbs, shrubs, and even the more visually attractive vegetables, such as carrots, beetroot, and red-leaved lettuce. Groups of roses of the same variety, well looked after, are useful additions to the shrub border and even the isolated favourite is acceptable in a small mixed bed; after all, it is the way the plants are combined together and their subsequent maintenance that matters rather than the actual choice of plants, provided they are suitable for your soil and climatic conditions.

Having put the two extremes of view forward, there are a number of other arguments both for and against underplanting which are not as often heard but are nonetheless valid.

On the side of the anti-underplanting lobby, there is the fact that hybrid tea and floribunda bush roses are highly bred and skilfully produced, and anything growing in competition with them is liable to have a detrimental effect on their well-being. There is no doubt that hybrid tea and floribunda roses (or what are now referred to under new nomenclature as large-flowered and cluster-flowered respectively) seem to thrive where the soil is clean beneath the bushes, but is this in part due to the fact that such beds are more likely to be tended by those keen rosarians who pay attention to other factors governing the health and good growth of the rose, such as correct pruning, spraying for pests and diseases, feeding, dead-heading and, most important, the right method of planting in the first place?

This point in itself raises other issues. Although the conventional bush roses still account for the majority of sales of new bushes, there is an increasing interest in both the 'old-fashioned' shrub and 'species' roses, such as 'Bourbon', 'Moss', 'Damask' and 'Musk'. These are much more informal of habit, simpler to prune, and lend themselves to being planted in single numbers, either in mixed borders or with other single varieties of shrub roses. Many of them are stronger-growing, often on their own rootstocks rather than budded, making it more possible for things to be planted beneath without detriment. In the past the drawback has been that some of these roses eventually grow too large for the smaller garden, restricting the choice to the smaller hybrid musks, like 'Buff Beauty', the common moss (*Rosa* × *centifolia* 'Muscosa'), and gallicas like 'Charles de Mills' and *Rosa* 'Mundi'.

In recent years a new breed of shrub rose, called the new English rose, has been developed. These roses have the characteristics, flower form and, in general, scent, of the 'old-fashioned' roses with the compactness and recurrent flowering habit of the modern hybrid teas and floribundas. They are suitable both for planting in quantity and as isolated specimens and, being of a much more informal appearance, can be underplanted without detracting from their looks; indeed, it can often contribute something to the scheme if suitable ground cover is introduced. If you should consider this possibility, it is essential that you choose the right varieties, as not all English roses are strong-growing enough to take the competition without some check to performance. Those most likely to come up smiling are 'Gertrude Jekyll' (deep pink), 'Graham Thomas' (yellow), 'Leander' (apricot, and very strong-growing), 'Heritage' (much smaller, shell-pink), 'Mary Rose' (flesh-coloured), and her crimson sport, 'William Shakespeare'.

There is, however, one very good reason why ground cover under roses is not a good idea, and that is the question of maintenance. Roses need feeding regularly to produce the healthiest growth and best blooms, and a thick mat of undergrowth makes it difficult – almost impossible – to apply dry fertilizers accurately and efficiently. Of course, there is always the alternative of foliar feeding, and this is quite acceptable, but must be done regularly and at the correct dilution, whereas a powder or granular feed only needs to be applied to the soil once or twice a season.

When the soil underneath rose bushes is densely covered another problem arises: garden hygiene. In some years the disease black spot is so rife and so virulent that, in spite of regular spraying, even the toughest roses eventually succumb and subsequently suffer partial or total defoliation. One of the ways in which black spot can be prevented from overwintering in the vicinity of the plants is to clear up all affected leaves at regular intervals, preferably burning them. Ground cover makes it just about impossible to do this thoroughly, and so spores can remain there until the next season, adding to any new airborne infection. There are some roses, such as the old favourite 'Peace', 'Chicago Peace', 'Prima Ballerina', and the newer 'Silver Jubilee', which are little affected by black spot, and so these are clearly the ones to think about if you do want to use ground cover.

There is no doubt, however, that roses during winter are not the most attractive of garden plants, especially those which are subjected to formal pruning once or twice a year, and so anything which can be done to brighten up the ground underneath between the months of, say, October and April is very welcome. Ground cover during the summer really is not necessary, as the canopy of leaves hides most of the soil anyway. Unfortunately, in this country it is virtually impossible to find plants, other than bulbs, which do something during the darkest months of the year and then obligingly disappear when the roses start to look interesting. The nearest thing I have ever seen is a planting of *Colchicum autumnale,* the autumn crocus, which flowers in September and October and then produces leaves which gradually die back as the weather warms up during the following season, but I have to say that apart from being green, broad and shiny, colchicum leaves do not have a lot going for them.

There is the point that I have been making throughout this book that anything which covers the ground is a form of ground cover, and in my garden, one could almost class crocuses as such, as they were planted thickly under my rose bushes when these were new, and have increased by division and seed ever since, until they are so close together you can hardly see the soil between on a sunny day when they are in full flower. Then when the flowers have faded, the leaves continue to increase in size to make very effective coverage until the new leaves of the roses take over, and I scarcely ever find a weed in that particular bed. When the leaves begin to die back, you do not notice them, because the young rose leaves are such a pretty colour that they draw your eyes away.

I manage to achieve a long flowering season by using the early 'species' forms like 'Blue Bird', 'Cream Beauty' and *tommasinianus*, and follow these with the larger flowered Dutch Hybrids, so in a mild season like the start of 1988 I had a good display from early January to the end of April.

As far as I know, you cannot use any other bulbs in quite the same way. Daffodils and narcissi grow too tall and their leaves are very untidy when the flowers have gone – they can nearly choke smaller rose varieties. Snowdrops are over too soon to be interesting. Tulips need more sun and flower too late to be of any use, and the leaves do not make good ground cover anyway, apart from perhaps hybrids from the wild, dwarfer forms like 'Red Riding Hood'. Scillas and chionodoxas have untidy leaves. Hyacinths are too formal; grape hyacinths (muscari) too invasive and too untidy out of flower.

As it is likely, therefore, that anything you choose as ground cover under roses will still be around when the roses are in full flight, suitable plants must be capable of retaining some interest while not detracting from the main purpose of the planting, which is the beauty of the roses themselves. They will also have to perform well in shade, as the area under well-grown rose bushes can be quite dark, especially where stronger-growing varieties have been planted or if they have been placed close together. Also, you do not want anything which is going to get tall and interfere with the growth of the roses, especially as far as the ripening of the wood of the new shoots goes as there could be a problem with frost damage. The roots must not penetrate too deeply and prevent the development of those of the roses.

There are fewer than half-a-dozen plants which I have tried in my own garden and which I have found to be moderately successful. One is *Viola labradorica*, which I have already described fully on page 76. This is not affected by shade, the leaves are of a pleasant purplish colour, and there always seem to be some violet-coloured flowers around; even as I write, which is mid-November, I can see some peeping through the leaves of the plants near my window. I have written at length about the invasive characteristics of this plant, but provided you are strict about removing any seedlings you do not want as soon as you notice them, this plant can make a good subject for cover under roses. In fact, all violets could be considered, but most of them do not have such a long flowering season, and the green leaves are not as interesting.

If you want variety, you could try contrasting *Viola labradorica* with a plant with some yellow in the leaves, and two which have done well for me under roses are the golden form of creeping Jenny, *Lysmachia nummularia* 'Aurea' (see page 44) and the variegated form of *Saxifraga urbium*, London Pride (see page 72). Of these two, I think the former is the more appropriate, as it is completely prostrate, the yellow flowers being produced along the trailing stems. For this purpose, the variegated London Pride would be better if it did not flower at all, as the pink sprays tend to be too tall and get muddled up with the stems of the roses, and for the sake of tidiness they need to be trimmed off after flowering.

Among the more compact shrub roses, *Vinca minor,* the lesser periwinkle, makes quite good ground cover under roses (especially the variegated forms), but once it is growing strongly it has to be watched, as it can grow up into the branches of the roses and, apart from looking untidy and interfering with the growth of these, once it gets really well entwined the job of removing it can be very painful.

One other plant which makes quite pretty ground cover, and which can be used in this kind of situation, is the variegated form of white clover, *Trifolium album* 'Purpureum', which has flowers like a wild white clover, much beloved of bees, but the leaves, many of which have four lobes, are a much more positive shade of green and the centres are shaded maroon-purple. It spreads rapidly by creeping stems, but requires the roses not to be planted too closely as the clover can become rather washed-out and straggly otherwise.

Even rosarian purists have been known to consent to edgings to the beds and borders, and these too are really another way in which ground cover is used. To be successful, the plants should be compact, maybe cushion-forming, and have a leaf shape which is pleasant when the plant is out of flower. Many of the low-growing perennials suggested in the chapter on ground cover for open areas (pages

Trifolium album 'Purpureum'

35–49) are suitable, even if they are only early flowering or have a short season at the start of summer, like aubretia, arabis, mossy saxifrages and the like, as you will not see the lack of flower once the roses start; all you require is a neat edging, such as that achieved by a close planting of the thrift or sea pink, *Armeria maritima*.

Grey-leaved perennials are particularly attractive as an edging to a rose bed. One of my earliest gardening memories is the edging of *Nepeta mussinii* (catmint) in my aunt's country garden. This produces its blue flowers along spikes of grey-green leaves all summer. Nepeta can get a little untidy and floppy when in full growth, so it should not be planted too near the edge of the lawn, which can become spoilt if the nepeta is allowed to lie on it for too long. The appearance of the edging can be improved by cutting it back to the base a couple of times a summer; it will soon shoot and come into flower again. The plants should be spaced at intervals of 12–15 inches (30–38 cm).

The other successful rose bed edging plant of which I have pleasant memories is the garden pink, dianthus. In the tougher days of my life when I would do most things to earn a crust, I did some jobbing gardening and routine maintenance work to supplement my scanty income as a garden designer, and one of the pleasanter contracts was for an old lady with the most delightful cottage garden, where every bed was thickly edged with pinks. I think they were 'Mrs Sinkins' (white), and 'Pink Mrs Sinkins', and the smell was heavenly. The chore of cutting the plants hard back after flowering, which prevents them from getting woody and bare at the base, was not quite so pleasant, and after a large sherry one particular lunchtime I nearly succeeded in removing the fleshy part of my thumb when work recommenced!

Pinks in flower seem to complement rather than detract from the roses, so for maximum benefit, it is a good idea to choose the modern hybrids like 'Doris' (pink) and 'Haytor' (white), which remain in flower throughout the summer. Spacing for these is 12 inches (30 cm) apart.

Roses as ground cover

You will have gathered from the preceding chapter that it is not impossible to use ground cover with roses, but roses can, in fact, also be used as ground cover themselves. The average bush rose is not suitable, of course, but there are certain forms which make very efficient and vandal-resistant cover for an open, sunny position, and it is interesting to see how many local authorities and other public bodies are turning to this form of cover when planting up large areas with ease of maintenance in mind.

Using roses as ground cover is not new. For many years the more lax and pliable ramblers have been recommended for this purpose. The most suitable varieties are those which throw up a good many long shoots from near the base, but which do not – unless you have vast acres to deal with – put on so much growth that they become unmanageable. This rather knocks on the head such otherwise admirable varieties as the white forms 'Bobbie James', 'Wedding Day' and *Rosa filipes* 'Kiftsgate', which are capable of spreading for 25 feet (8 m) or more.

The best ones to look out for are what is known as the 'Wichuraiana Hybrids' which have been bred from a species called *Rosa wichuraiana*. This originated in the Far East and has a naturally scrambling or prostrate habit without producing excessive growth, and it has proved a good parent of such old favourites as the creamy 'Alberic Barbier'; 'Albertine' (coppery-pink); 'American Pillar' (carmine pink with a white eye); 'Crimson Shower', which is a fairly new red variety flowering later than most ramblers and being slightly less prone to mildew than some of them are; the pink 'Dorothy Perkins'; 'Emily Gray' (buff-yellow); 'Excelsa', which looks like a red form of 'Dorothy Perkins'; and 'New Dawn', a repeat-flowering 'sport' (mutation) of the pink 'Dr W van Fleet', which is useful in that it does not just have one flush of flowers and then nothing else for the rest of the summer.

To use these roses as ground cover, you may find that all you need to do in the way of training is to plant them in a favourable spot in

THE BIG COVER-UP

ground enriched with well-rotted farmyard manure to encourage the rapid production of long, strong shoots, and then leave them to their own devices. However, if they are growing exceptionally well, they may need help to lie flat, as some of the branches will set off skywards for quite a while before they become so long that they start to bend over of their own volition. Pegging them down also helps to position each stem where you want it – that is, filling in the bare pieces of ground. I find that the cheapest and easiest way to do this is to cut an old wire coat-hanger – straightened out first, of course! – into pieces about 8 inches (20 cm) or so long, which can then be bent in the middle and pegged over the stems so they are secured to the ground. If you have difficulty in cutting thick wire like that of which metal coat hangers are made, I suggest you obtain a pair of 'hobby shears', which cut through even quite thick metal easily (see page 142).

I cannot say with all honesty, however, that rambler roses are particularly labour-saving when used as ground cover; they do require a certain amount of care and maintenance if they are to look their best. For a start, it is more important that they receive regular feeding than it is with most other suitable subjects. This can be difficult to apply, except as a foliar feed given fortnightly throughout the growing and flowering season, which may not appeal to many people. Then there is the decided drawback that, apart from 'Crimson Shower', most ramblers of *Rosa wichuraiana* origin get an appalling amount of mildew most summers, and regular spraying for this has to commence as soon as the first few leaf buds start to unfurl to stand any chance at all of control. I find that 'Tumbleblite' is about the most effective chemical for this purpose, and as greenfly can also be a problem, you can add 'Tumblebug' to it when you spray, but as both these products have a degree of persistence (which is why they are so effective), if you are not keen on the use of such chemicals on a regular basis, you may, in fact, ask yourself whether this is the best form of ground cover you can plant.

Perhaps the best use for ramblers as cover is when they are planted at the top of a steep bank; with some initial formative training, they will cascade down to give a profusion of summer flowers. But here again, apart from the remontant (repeat-flowering) 'New Dawn' and 'Alberic Barbier', which, after its first flush, has a few flowers until the frosts, the flowering season is a comparatively short one, and after the flowers are over, once the bushes are established, you could be in for some hard work, as *wichuraiana* ramblers will not go on for ever without some pruning and general tidying up.

Where a rambler is grown over a pergola or fence, it benefits from having those shoots which have flowered, or at least a proportion of them, removed immediately the blooms have faded. This keeps the plant tidy and encourages the production of new wood which will flower the following season. While it is not quite as important to do this every year when the ramblers are being used as ground cover, as you do not mind if the individual plants spread over quite a wide area, they will eventually need the oldest branches taken out to promote young growth, which usually has the best flower trusses on it. This can be both an awkward and a painful job, and it is tempting to ignore it until the planting is screaming out for attention, when it begins to resemble a barbed-wire barricade with leaves.

On the other hand, if you choose a strongly scented variety, such as 'Albertine', few other forms of ground cover will give you the same pleasure on a warm summer's evening. I certainly would not discount rambler roses as a viable form of cover – you just have to be aware of the shortcomings and accept that aesthetically they can be one of the best subjects to use – but they are not the least demanding regarding care and maintenance.

There is a different type of rose, however, which has come very much to the fore in recent times, and that is the prostrate, arching or spreading, shrubby sort, which combines moderate growth habit with a long flowering period, ease of cultivation and dense, weed-smothering foliage, and it is this kind which is now so popular with local councils and landscape architects.

Some of the roses which fit into this category have been around a long time, and these are small, spreading and prostrate shrub roses, like the 'Dunwich Rose', hybrids of *Rosa rugosa* like 'Frau Dagmar Hastrup', 'Hansa', 'Moje Hammarberg', 'Max Graf' and 'Red Max Graf'; *R. nitida* and *R. paulii*. Until their potential was realized as ideal ground- cover plants, they had featured in gardens more as individual plants or small groups, or as part of a larger collection of shrub roses, but, correctly spaced, there is no doubt that they make excellent weed-smothering cover, while not requiring the same looking after as ramblers used for the same purpose. This is not to say that some attention is not needed; they will, naturally, require feeding, although given good soil and a sunny position, an annual application of a specific rose fertilizer worked among the bare branches in early spring is usually adequate. They also tend to be more resistant to diseases like mildew and black spot, so in favourable years no action need be taken unless the diseases actually begin to show themselves.

Other roses which are useful for ground-cover schemes have been specially bred in the last few years specifically for the purpose. The first introduction which has proved itself so successful as a carpeting rose is 'Nozomi', a pale pink, prostrate rose which flowers continuously in summer for about two months, then produces a spreading mass of stems covered in small, glossy, green leaves. 'Nozomi' is still popular as a ground-cover rose, but has been joined by many more, some of which are far superior in both growth habit and flower form, but for ease of cultivation and strength of growth, I feel it will continue to be a favourite for many years to come.

Some of the more strong-growing forms, like *Rosa* × *paulii* and the 'Gamebird' series of modern ground-cover roses which are named after sporting birds, will cover a large area of ground with a single plant and are therefore equal to ramblers in function, but require less training and cultivation. Many are capable of producing roots along the branches where they touch the soil, and so provide a viable alternative to the plants suggested in the chapter on ground cover for binding loose earth, on pages 82–95.

Ground-cover roses are also handy for covering low eyesores like shabby dwarf walls, tree stumps, manhole covers, septic tanks and the like. Their main disadvantage is that they lose their leaves in winter, but this drawback is offset in certain varieties by attractive autumn colouring and, birds permitting, brightly coloured hips, as in the case of some of the *Rosa rugosa* hybrids.

While some maintenance may be necessary, this is usually confined to a general tidying of the planting and the removal of any old branches which have become unsightly or unproductive.

Perhaps the greatest advantage of using roses as ground cover is on the basis of cost, as unlike many plants whose success in weed suppression is proportional to the denseness of the young specimens, most carpeting roses can be positioned comparatively wide apart, thus cutting down considerably the quantities needed.

Lysmachia nummularia **'Aurea' and** *Viola labradorica* **growing under roses**
A mass planting of crocuses covering the ground of an otherwise bare rose bed

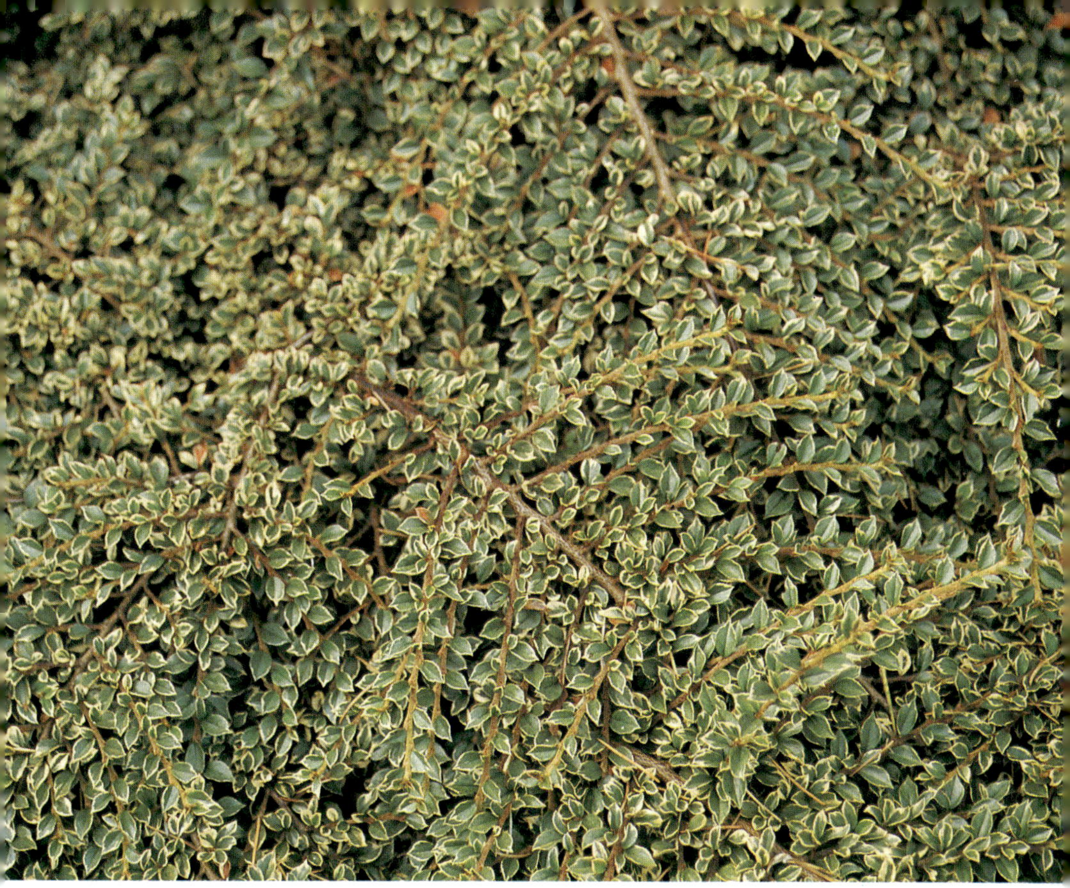

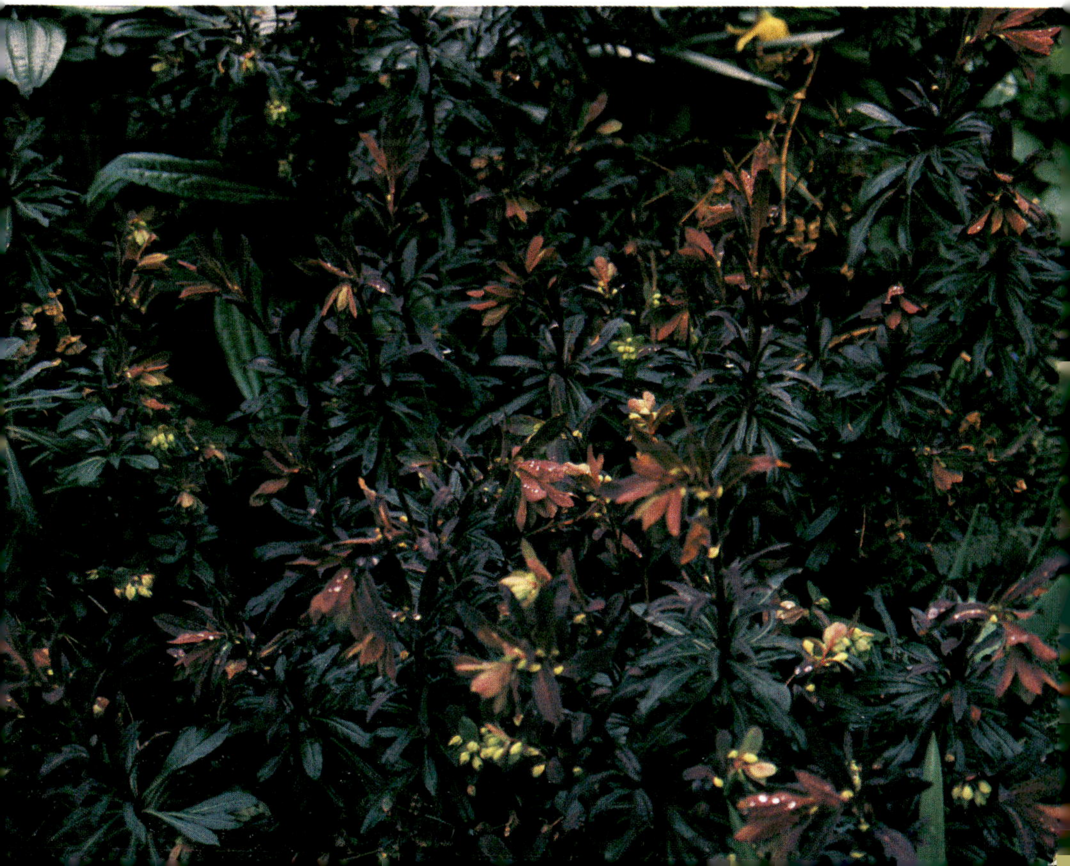

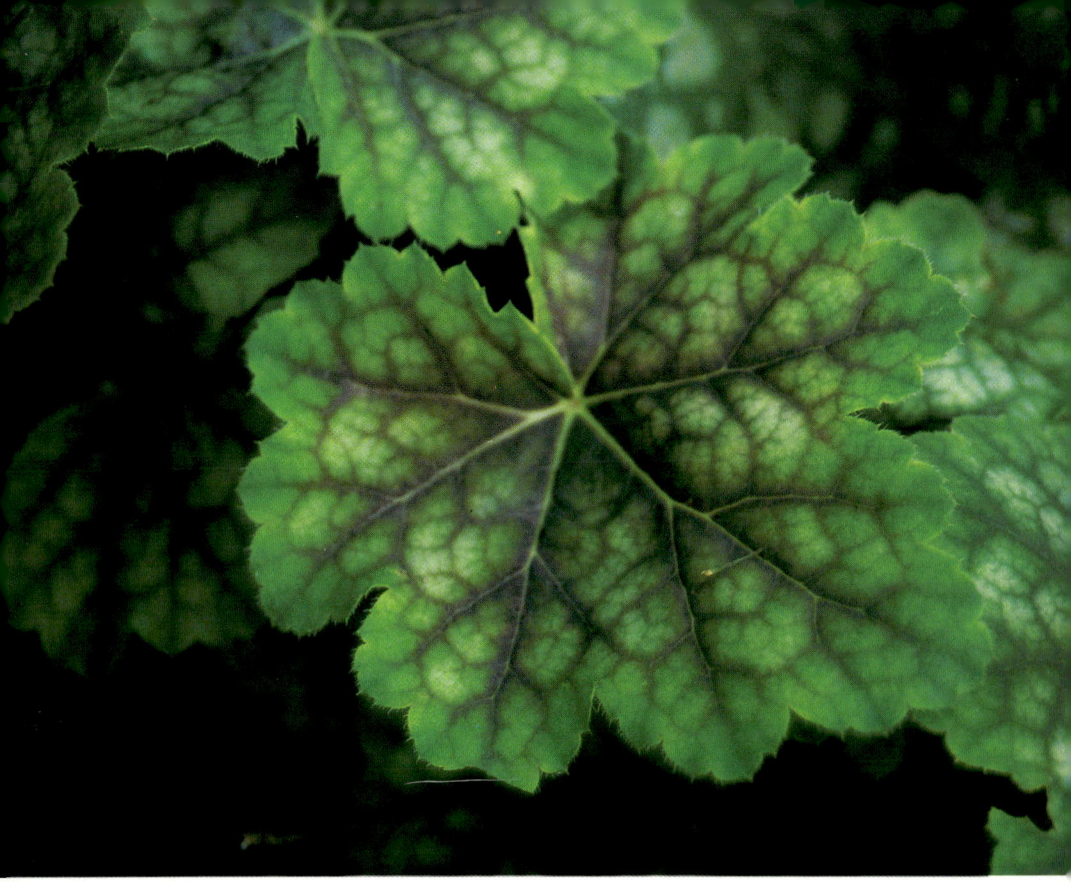

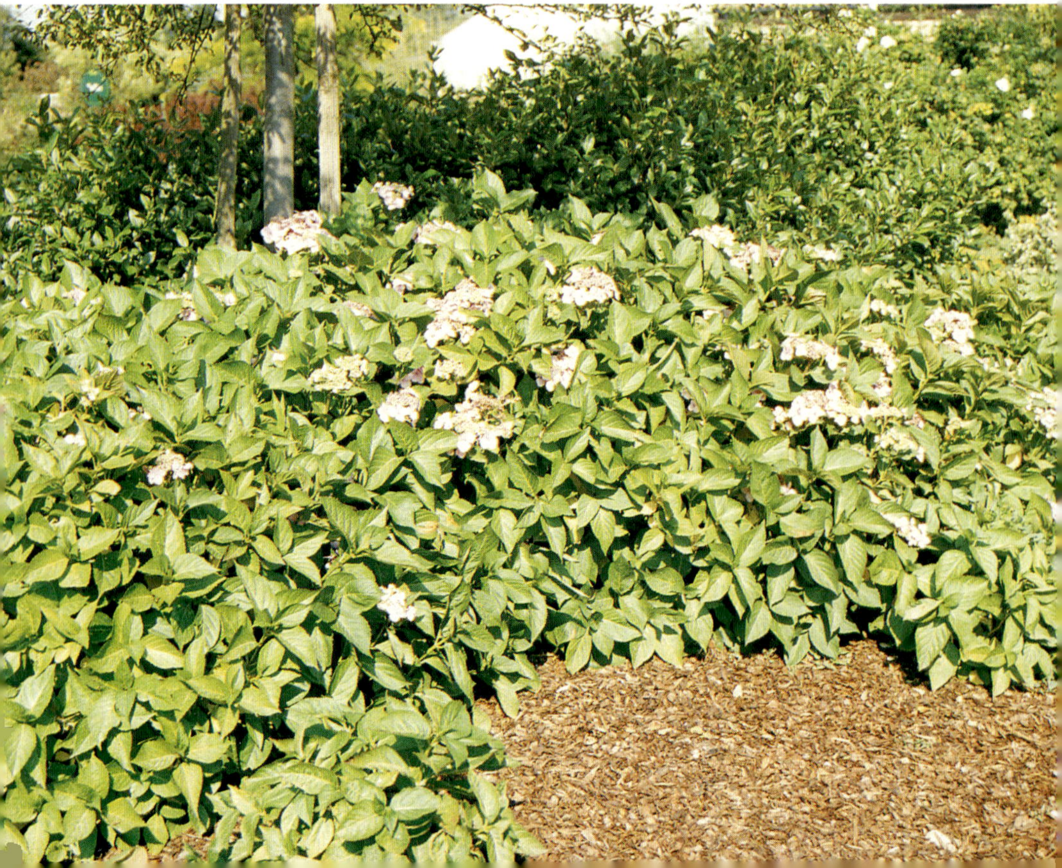

ROSES AS GROUND COVER

When buying ground-cover roses, it is advisable to ascertain whether or not they are grown on their own rootstocks. With most varieties, it is not only possible to do this, but also desirable, as when they have been budded onto another rootstock, suckering can occur, both spoiling the effect and seriously complicating the maintenance of the planting. In years to come, when micropropagation of roses is the norm rather than the exception, there should be even less difficulty in obtaining adequate numbers of a wide range of good quality bushes growing on their own roots.

These are the roses which I have found to make the most effective cover, but I realize that the list is by no means comprehensive, and many others can be added, especially suckering or thicket-forming shrub roses which grow taller. *Rosa rugosa* itself is a typical example, and I shall be mentioning this again later on page 137. If you are thinking of experimenting with roses as ground cover, perhaps the best advice I can offer is to see any variety you think might be a good subject growing, not in the nursery, but as you would find it in the normal garden. Some nurseries have excellent display gardens where you can see many of the modern and species shrub roses and ground-cover varieties growing (see page 141). The trial grounds of The Royal National Rose Society, Chiswell Green, St Albans, Herts should also provide you with all you want to know about the habit of most roses likely to make suitable ground cover.

Suitable roses widely available

'Bonica' is one of the newer varieties, and is a mound-forming plant rather than prostrate. The bushes are well covered right to the base and so at the correct spacing – 4 feet (1.2 m) – it makes a very dense spread. The young leaves are particularly attractive as they are a coppery colour, eventually becoming dark green, glossy and leathery. The flowers are pale pink, maturing a brighter colour, and semi-double. Eventual height is about 3 feet (1 m), the branches arching over to make a canopy. Flowers are usually produced from June until September.

The 'Dunwich Rose' was originally a wild species, growing on Dunwich beach in Suffolk. It grows about 2 feet (60 cm) tall, and has

---

The variegated form of London Pride can be used in rose beds
Ajuga **'Burgundy Glow' will grow almost anywhere**

a suckering habit which makes it handy for binding loose earth. It has single, white flowers. Plants should be spaced about 2 feet (60 cm) apart.

'Ferdy' is another newish shrub with the most delightful flowers – fuchsia-pink and double, opening to show a creamy centre. The main flush is produced in June, and there is usually another in September, the blooms having a sweet scent. The bush is of arching habit, growing to about 3 feet (1 m), with fine leaves. Space plants 3 feet (1 m) apart.

'Fiona' is nice, because in addition to its deep red flowers produced in succession from early summer, it also produces hips, and has red-tinted young leaves in spring. The habit is similar to 'Ferdy', but the bushes are wider-spreading, reaching about 4½ feet (1.5 m) in time. Plant 'Fiona' at 3–foot (1–m) intervals.

I have used 'Frau Dagmar Hastrup' (also 'Frau Dagmar Hartopp') for many years for ground cover, long before its use became fashionable. It is a low-growing hybrid of *Rosa rugosa,* with single pink flowers opening from real 'rosebud-shaped' buds. As the flowers fade, very large, round hips form which you can make rose-hip syrup with if the birds do not get there first. There is a long flowering season, and in autumn the foliage turns yellow before falling to expose the hips on the bare branches. The ultimate height is a little under 3 feet (1 m). The plants should be spaced 2–2½ feet (60–80 cm) apart.

'Grouse' is a prostrate, wide-spreading rose, covering up to 12 feet (3–4 m) eventually. It grows about 12 inches (30 cm) high, and has a profusion of pale pink, scented flowers and glossy green leaves. Similar in habit to 'Grouse' is 'Pheasant' (light pink with double flowers), and 'Partridge' (white blooms, single or semi-double). Space at intervals of 4 feet (1.2 m).

'Hansa' is another *Rosa rugosa* hybrid, growing taller than 'Frau Dagmar Hastrup' to about 5 feet (1.5 m) with heavily fragrant, double flowers of reddish-violet through the summer followed by large red hips. Space plants 2–2½ feet (60–80 cm) apart. Similar, but with larger flowers, is 'Moje Hammarberg' and the slightly taller still 'Roserie de l'Hay'.

'Max Graf' is an interesting rose, because it is a hybrid between *R. rugosa* and *R. wichuraiana,* and with the inherited characteristics from both, it makes admirable ground cover, forming thickets about 2 feet (60 cm) tall, spreading over a wide area. The flowers are heavily

ROSES AS GROUND COVER

scented, bright pink and produced in large numbers in June and July, but not after that, unfortunately. The leaves are shiny and well clothe the prostrate or semi-prostrate stems, which themselves can root along their length and so help to bind banks and other areas of loose soil. 'Max Graf' is thought to be the first ground-cover rose as such, being bred in the USA in 1919. Space plants 3 feet (1 m) apart.

Rosa nitida is a thicket-forming rose which gets ever wider. There are scented, single pink flowers in early summer, followed by brightly coloured hips, and the stems are of a pleasing warm brown shade which looks good when the leaves have fallen. Initial spacing is 2–3 feet (60 cm–1 m) apart.

'Nozomi' is technically classed as a climbing miniature, but it is usually listed in catalogues as a shrub. It is a Japanese rose and its pink flowers are widely seen in public parks and other municipal urban spaces. It is not as lax as the 'gamebird' roses, and may need some initial help in getting it to lie flat and cover the places it is supposed to cover. Space plants 2–3 feet (60 cm–1 m) apart.

Rosa × paulii is a very old shrub rose, which makes superb cover for areas liable to be vandalized, as it makes thick hummocks of long, trailing, well-clothed, horribly thorny branches. The flowers are unusual, with crinkled petals, white, with yellow stamens, which have a heavy scent of cloves. One plant will spread many feet, so the spacing can be up to 5 feet (1.5 m) apart. Again there is the drawback that this species only flowers in midsummer, but it is such a tough, obliging rose that I suppose you cannot have everything.

'Pink Bells', 'Red Bells' and 'White Bells' are three very similar roses, only differing from each other in the colour of the flowers. They all have an arching growth habit and will reach a height of about 2–2½ feet (60–80 cm) by about 4 feet (1.2 m) across. The flowers are double, quite small, and appear for about two months from mid-July. Like most of these modern ground-cover varieties, the foliage is attractive and shiny. Space plants 2½–3 feet (80 cm–1 m) apart.

'Pink Drift' is, in my opinion, one of the best of the stronger-growing prostrate roses. Height and spread is about the same as 'Grouse' and spacing about 3–4 feet (1–1.2 m) apart, but the flowers are pale pink and double and the season is not quite as long.

'Pink Wave' is an arching shrub rose, reaching about 3 feet (1 m) tall by 4 feet (1.2 m) across. It produces its double pink flowers for

THE BIG COVER-UP

about three months from June. Space plants 3 feet (1 m) apart.

'Red Blanket', 'Rosy Cushion' and 'Smarty' are another three very similar varieties, and have been around some time as ground-cover roses. 'Red Blanket' has small, scented, red, semi-double flowers, those of 'Rosy Cushion' are rose-pink with a white centre, while the blooms of 'Smarty' are single pink. All three are perpetual-flowering, and the growth is vigorous, healthy, semi-prostrate and dense, the foliage being retained for a large part of the winter, thus making them first-rate weed-suppressing varieties. Plant at 3–feet (1–m) intervals.

'Red Max Graf' is similar to its pink counterpart, but the habit is not as strong. The flowers are large, single and bright red, and the plants should be spaced rather closer together than 'Max Graf', at a distance of about 2½ feet (80 cm).

'Snow Carpet' is the perfect ground-cover rose for the confined space or small garden, as it reaches a mere 6 inches (15 cm) in height, and a fully-grown plant will spread less than 3 feet (1 m). It is completely prostrate, with small, ferny leaves and pure white double flowers all summer. Space plants 18 inches (45 cm) apart. Another ground-cover rose for the more restricted border is also white. 'Swany' is slightly taller, and can grow up to about 12 inches (30 cm) tall in good soil, but the habit of this one, too, is virtually prostrate. Spacing is 2 feet (60 cm) apart.

'The Fairy' is a shrub rose which was introduced in 1932, although its worth as a ground-cover plant was discovered much more recently than that. It is, in fact, a polyantha rose, and one of the few to survive in general cultivation. It has small, neat, glossy leaves and the mass of blooms start to appear in late July when the summer has warmed up a bit. The flowers are coral-pink, small, double, and vaguely reminiscent of those of the rambler 'Dorothy Perkins'. The bushes are of spreading habit, growing to about 3 feet (1 m) by 4 feet (1.2 m) and it is extremely tough and hardy. Space plants at intervals of 2½ feet (80 cm).

Using climbers as ground cover

When I began writing this book I was in two minds whether to include a chapter on climbers or not, because my own feelings are that if you want an effective and labour-saving ground cover, there are many more plants which would do the job better than those we normally think of as climbers. I did, however, persuade myself that the book would not be comprehensive without some words on the idea, if only to put forward the pros and cons and help to clear up the confusion which can occur in people's minds when they read other literature on the subject.

Very early on in my gardening career, I saw a 'whimsy' article – I forget by whom, which is possibly just as well! – advocating the use of rampant climbers to cover large, bare patches of earth, rather after the fashion of using rambler roses, only more so. I have never been fortunate enough, or unfortunate, maybe, to have so much ground that I have needed to swallow up a huge portion of it with just one plant, but during my life as a working landscape gardener, I did receive occasional requests for this form of ground cover, so I have had a chance to play around with the idea, and my conclusion is that it does work, but I certainly do not think that in the majority of cases it looks as good as employing more conventional plants. It definitely is not the 'plant it and forget it' idea, requiring in general much more regular attention, and there are periods in the year when the cover looks boring, at best.

On the other hand, if you really have got acres of ground, and you are looking for a new effect, then climbers are worth trying, although you must be prepared for quite a lot of initial training, and especially regular pruning once the scheme is underway, to keep the area looking at its neatest. I am still of the opinion that this kind of planting belongs to the same stable as the theory that an uninteresting privet hedge can be brightened up by growing rambling plants through it – suggestions like this always make me wonder whether

THE BIG COVER-UP

the advocate has had any practical experience of gardening at all, or they would know that to keep the thing neat thereafter you either lose the bits of the climber which you want to retain, or you ignore the ever-increasing growth of the hedge. Either way, it only partly works, and the end result is not as good as the neatly trimmed privet anyway, and not even as aesthetic as a decent brick wall!

There is, though, one very good instance where the idea can be the most practical solution to a difficult problem, and that is where the ground is so poor that to plant it all over with ground cover would entail an enormous amount of prior preparation – it may not be practicable to do this anyway – or where a bank or cutting is so steep it would be unwise to disturb it, or it would be impossible to put on enough topsoil to give the plants the sort of start they need to get them growing and joining up quickly, which is the whole object of the exercise. In this case, it may be possible to improve isolated areas, excavating out and disposing of the rubbish and introducing some good soil into which the plant can get a good hold so it soon romps away and hides the rest of the area.

The excavation would have to be adequately large, and deep enough – at least 4–5 feet (1.2–1.5 m) in diameter by 2 feet (60 cm) deep – or the roots will come up against poor soil too quickly, which will begin to check the top growth. Where a bank is involved, it is usually wiser to make the improvement either at the top or the bottom, depending on which is the more practical, in order not to damage its stability. The plants you select would then need to be capable either of climbing or scrambling up or of trailing down according to whether it has to be planted at the bottom of the slope or where it has levelled out at the top.

While the main plan is to cover the earth and both improve its appearance and restrict weed growth (weeds, I am afraid, will have a go at getting established in just about anything, even if their subsequent performance is less than first-rate), many climbing plants, especially those which normally cling by modified roots with suckers, will produce ordinary soil roots if they are allowed to sprawl over the earth and do not come up against anything solid, so in time certain species will stabilize soil and get a tidier hold on it. This is especially so where the shoots have been pegged down to the ground during training, and is encouraged by covering the peg with a little good soil in order to bury the stem at that point. I find again that the best

USING CLIMBERS AS GROUND COVER

material for making 'staples' is the ubiquitous wire coathanger, cut up into lengths as described on page 104 and bent in the middle. Alternatively, it is sometimes possible to make them by bending bamboo canes, though these often split completely, and there are some shrubs, like willow and hazel, which produce pliable, thin branches that can be bent and twisted to form pegs, rather in the way that a thatcher uses hazel spars for securing straw to a roof. Do make sure if you are using, say, willow or poplar – another tree which provides long, flexible growths if 'pollarded' (cut hard back to the main trunk) – that you strip the bark off completely before use, or you will find that, instead of ground cover, you could end up with a forest of unwanted saplings! It does not matter if these pegs rot after a season or two, as, with a bit of luck, the prostrate shoots of the climber should have 'layered' themselves, the new roots holding firmly to the ground.

Sometimes the effect can be improved if you grow two species together, in the same way that it is often possible to do this on a wall or a trellis. You can then combine interesting foliage and attractive flowers, as it is not often that you will be able to have both on the same plant. It is important to make sure that the two species you are using are capable of withstanding the same pruning treatment – for example, a large-flowered hybrid clematis flowering after midsummer can be cut back as hard as you like and combines well with, for example, parthenocissus (Virginia creeper), which can also be pruned severely without it losing any of the attraction of the leaves, either in summer or when they colour up in autumn, whereas if you were to combine parthenocissus with a very early-flowering form of clematis and you wished to trim the parthenocissus back every autumn, you would cut the flowering shoots off your clematis as well.

Climbing plants suitable for pegging down or allowing to ramble untrained as ground cover

A purely ornamental form of the Chinese gooseberry, **Actinidia kolomikta** has large, heart-shaped leaves with a rough surface which are delightfully variegated cream and pink once the plant has matured. The stems are stiff, branching and may need some assistance initially to cover and remain close to the ground where you want them to. Although deciduous, it has a tidy habit and will require little pruning or routine attention, though, if possible, the winter appearance is improved by picking off the discarded leaves. It combines well with early flowering clematis hybrids such as 'The President' which also need minimal pruning. In time, one plant will cover up to 13 feet (4 m), though for speed of coverage, individual plants may be spaced at 6-foot (2 m) intervals. Where bank cover is required, it is better to position the plants at the base and allow them to climb up, as the habit does not lend itself to 'draping'. Sunny, open positions are best.

Aristolochia macrophylla (Dutchman's pipe) is a vigorous twiner with very big, kidney-shaped leaves and curious, pitcher-shaped pendulous flowers of a yellowish-green and brown produced in June and July. Some initial framework may be necessary to encourage the correct spread, but this can merely be of thick wire attached to short stakes. Once the plant has covered these, it will largely cover the ground by climbing round itself. Usually only one plant is necessary as coverage will soon attain 20 feet (6 m) or more. Some rooting along the stems may take place but it is not usual. It can look very untidy in time and there will come the day when severe pruning will be essential, but the cut stems will easily regrow. It is not a good idea to grow anything else in conjunction with this plant, because of the amount of growth it makes. It is suitable for any aspect.

Akebia quinata, another twiner, is not as overbearing as the last one, even though its growth is as rapid. Initial training is similar. The leaves are smallish and five-lobed and after small, maroon flowers in spring, strange, fleshy, brown, sausage-shaped fruits can be found in a good season. A south or west aspect is best. Coverage is about the same, or ultimately slightly more, than that achieved by Dutchman's pipe, and both of these will hide an unsightly bank if planted either at the top or the bottom. It will thicken up if cut hard back every second year or so.

Campsis grandiflora (trumpet vine) is sprawling climber which will cover about the same amount of ground in favourable conditions if given a warm, sunny spot. Flowers, which are orange and trumpet-shaped, are borne in panicles on growth produced in the current season. Treatment of the young plants and after-care is similar to the two above. If used to cover a bank, it produces a better effect if positioned at the bottom.

Celastrus scandens is yet another rapid twiner which should be treated in a similar way to the two above for ground-cover purposes.

USING CLIMBERS AS GROUND COVER

The leaves colour up well in autumn and orange seed vessels open to expose bright red seeds. As the plant gets older, it may become bare in the centre if young shoots are not encouraged to twine into this and cover it up. Some clipping back may be necessary to keep it within bounds which will thicken up the cover.

There are many **clematis** which can be employed as ground cover. Possibly the best plant with which to cover any eyesore, whether at ground level or not, is the rampant *Clematis montana* and its various pink cultivars such as 'Rubens', Elizabeth', 'Freda', 'Marjorie', 'Mayleen', 'Pink Perfection' and 'Tetra-rose'. These all have pleasantly-shaped, thick, bronze-tinted foliage and a profusion of flowers in spring, followed by a forest of fast-growing new shoots which will twine around each other and anything else they can get hold of. Using this as ground cover is certainly not a good idea if you are keen on tidiness, as it is chaotic both in growth and in dormancy, but it certainly does a terrific job of smothering everything else.

When growth begins to get completely out of hand, the whole area can be tipped back in late summer, but not too much must be removed or you will take off the flowering stems for the following year. Eventually more severe action might have to be taken, going right back to the main stems or trunk; this should be done immediately after flowering to enable enough new growth to be produced to flower the following spring. Various other species forms, like *Clematis macropetala, C. viticella* and the yellow *C. tangutica* which also has 'old man's beard' seed heads in the autumn, can be used in a similar way.

For a more restricted area, you could use one of the many forms of late-flowering large-flowered hybrids, which, as I have already mentioned earlier, can be intertwined with other climbers to give additional interest to the scheme. These can be kept in check by cutting back to the roots, or to a main branch framework, every winter. It would be difficult to single out suitable varieties as much would depend on colour preference, but for a small piece of ground you could try the red-crimson 'Rouge Cardinal' which always seems to produce plenty of foliage, or the pink, undemanding 'Comtesse de Bouchard', while if the space is larger, the stronger-growing 'Etoile Violette' (purple with yellow stamens), 'Huldine' (white with pale mauve bars on the reverse of the petals), 'Gipsy Queen' (violet-purple), Jackmanii and 'Jackmanii Superba' (purple), 'Jackmanii Alba'

THE BIG COVER-UP

Clematis 'Etoile Violette'

(white) and 'Jackmanii Rubra' (petunia red) will give good coverage. To encourage soil rooting along the stems, it is more favourable to position the pegs between the leaf joints rather than at them, as is the case with most climbing plants, as the biggest concentration of root-producing hormones is found internodally in the clematis.

The one serious drawback about using the large-flowered hybrid forms is the risk of their contracting clematis wilt. This is thought either to be a fungus, or a disorder affecting the conductive tissue when the plant is growing very rapidly and therefore under stress, and shows itself in the totally unexpected wilting, collapse and subsequent death of single stems or, where the disease is very severe, the whole plant. There is no real cure, but cutting the affected plants right back to the base, watering with a fungicide, then giving regular watering to which a dilute liquid feed has been added will sometimes result in the plants recovering and putting up new shoots. Clematis grown in moist, alkaline soil and well fed with a suitable fertilizer such as is sold for roses will ensure that they are being given the best growing conditions and, unlike most plants, burying the rootball deeper than it was originally when in its pot helps the formation of more roots, which also helps to keep the dreaded wilt at bay.

Hydrangea petiolaris, the climbing hydrangea, has aerial roots which cling to any hard surface, but if not provided with a support, it will form a low mound of widening growth, eventually spreading as much as 10 feet (3 m) wide. The white flowers are of the lacecap type, and appear in midsummer, and no pruning is required. It is perhaps one of the better climbers for ground cover purposes as it is neater of habit than most, and can be used in conjunction with some of the large-flowered clematis varieties to prolong the interest of the planting.

Many forms of **lonicera** (honeysuckle) will ramble over the ground but can look very untidy in winter if they are deciduous, although the scent is gorgeous. The early Dutch and late Dutch (**Lonicera** 'Begica' and 'Serotina' respectively) have very strong scents and can be planted together to ensure a continuity of flower from May to September. The individual stems will twist round each other usually to provide their own support, though some initial guidance may be necessary. Red berries are produced in the autumn which are attractive to a number of birds, particularly warblers such as lesser whitethroats and blackcaps. The plants should be positioned at the base of a bank and allowed to climb upwards, rather than at the top. For good evergreen cover, *L. japonica* 'Halliana' is perhaps the best, spreading up to 13 feet (4 m), with a mass of medium-sized, pale green, evergreen or semi-evergreen leaves and biscuit-coloured, sweetly scented flowers from June until the autumn. Pruning is only necessary if the structure begins to look bare or growth becomes excessive.

The **Virginia creepers** will ramble happily over the ground if no support is provided to climb up, occasionally producing roots along the stems, and they will make quite dense cover if the new shoots, which generally begin by growing directly upwards, are clipped off about two-thirds of the way along their length. While this cannot be classed as labour-saving gardening by any stretch of the imagination, the effect is certainly different, and it does not look too untidy in

THE BIG COVER-UP

Lonicera 'late Dutch'

winter if the dead leaves are raked off. The original Virginia creeper is *P. quinquefolia;* a more showy species is *P. henryana,* which has dark, velvety-green leaves with silver and pink veins. Possibly the form which colours up best in the autumn is *P. veitchii*. The spread of these creepers when they are allowed to run along the ground is infinite. If used for bank cover, the plants can be positioned either at the top or the bottom of the slope.

A close relation of parthenocissus is vitis, a genus which includes a number of ornamental vines. These are even faster-growing than the Virginia creepers and, being rather more lax, tend to be untidier, but will certainly cover an area quickly and are especially useful for a messy bank. *Vitis coignetiae* has huge leaves which turn brilliant orange and red shades in the autumn. There are small, sweetly scented flowers in early summer, followed by small, purple grapes. *V. vinifera*

'Purpurea' is a purple-leaved form of fruiting grape, and, although strong-growing, is more restrained than *V. coignetiae.*

Polygonum baldschuanicum (mile-a-minute or Russian vine) is well-known as just about the fastest thing on roots, and can reach a great height as a climber in a single season. This is one climbing plant I have actually used in my own garden in the past as ground cover. This was by accident, as it happened to be climbing up an old pear tree in my first real garden. The pear tree blew over, but the polygonum was not easily deterred, and all attempts to remove it by spraying it with weedkiller, digging it out, and even pouring paraffin over it and setting light to it in an attempt to burn it out proved to be of no avail. Eventually I gave in, and let it scramble down a rough, shaly incline where not much else would grow, clipping it back when it reached the limits of its allotted space. This thickened up the base of the plant and it made quite a pleasant feature, white, frothy panicles of flower appearing from July until September, though these were not as profuse as they would have been if it had been allowed to grow unchecked. It certainly was not a low-maintenance form of ground cover as it required as much clipping at its extremities as, say, a privet hedge would have done, but I have since had no hesitation in using it to cover one side of a cutting where only sub-soil remained and which was too steep to do much else with. It will either climb up or hang down, so it can have its uses.

The most appropriate area for **wistaria** to be used as ground cover is on a sloping site, preferably quite steep, so that it can be seen to its best advantage, with the flower trusses hanging down naturally. The most commonly offered form is *Wistaria sinensis:* this is a lovely plant with a somewhat deserved bad reputation as far as flowering is concerned, as some plants can take years before they produce trusses in any appreciable number; however, the wait is well worth it. If it is grown as a wall shrub, flowering can be encouraged sometimes by cutting back the current season's lateral growths to about 6 inches (15 cm) in July or August, and then again to two buds from the base in December, much as you would summer and winter prune an espalier apple tree. The reason for this is to attempt to encourage the formation of the short, spur-like growths which produce the flowers. However, if you are using the plant to cover the ground, you want as much growth as possible, and I find the best thing to do in such a case is to let nature take its course; flowers will definitely be produced in the fullness of time. One or two newer imports, like the white 'Domino', have been bred to encourage early flowering, but I find that the growth habit is not as satisfactory for ground cover. A very attractive, rapid-growing white species is *W. venusta,* which has very large trusses containing individually big flowers, and a covering of thick down on the young shoots and leaves. For a pink form, look for *W. floribunda* 'Rosea'.

The young stems will almost certainly have to be trained to fill the area you want them to, while they are still soft and pliant. If you are growing the wistaria to cover a bank, you should find that the top growth as it cascades over will amply hide the base, which will become woody and bare after a few years. If, however, you should decide to use the plant on the level, some of the young growths may have to be trained on to the older branches to cover them up. I do not really recommend this position, though, as the flower trusses will be partially hidden by the foliage and stems and the cascading effect will be lost.

Taller shrubs as ground cover

The general concept of ground-cover planting is the close positioning of lower-growing plants, but there is no reason at all why suitable taller shrubs should not be brought into use. Indeed, in larger schemes, or where whole areas of a garden have been designed for ultimate minimum maintenance, too many short species tend to give an undesirably flat effect, rather like using too many bedding plants without the introduction of taller varieties to lend height to the design. Larger shrubs with dense canopies, especially when planted closer together than the norm, will control weeds just as efficiently as carpeting ones, and provided they are planted in the right places from the outset, they should not require any more attention.

Unless your garden is particularly vast, it is better to combine taller and shorter plants – the more diminutive ones being placed on the outside of the bed or border, of course! – rather than use all taller ones, which are likely to dominate and look out of proportion. It is not necessary to use evergreen species exclusively, in fact, it is desirable to have some deciduous blocks to relieve the slightly 'cemetery' effect that too many evergreens are inclined to create.

Amelanchier lamarckii (snowy mespilus) has become popular in the last few years as a very effective plant for mass planting. Left to its own devices, it will form a small tree 20 feet (6 m) or more tall, but it can be trimmed back after flowering to keep it much shorter. It is a first-class multi-purpose shrub, with a froth of white flowers in spring as the pinkish-tinged leaves unfurl, fresh green foliage all summer, and superb autumn colour. For quick effect space plants 4 feet (1.2 m) apart, otherwise more space can be left between individual plants.

When **Aucuba japonica** (spotted laurel) is planted in a favourable position, it will grow much taller, denser and faster than in the type of area described on page 77. The colour will also be brighter and therefore a block planting of any of the variegated forms will provide interest and a contrast to species with darker leaves. Space plants 4 feet (1.2 m) apart for the best cover.

Berberis is a vast genus, all members of which can be considered as ground-cover plants. Of the deciduous species, any of the taller-growing forms of *B. thunbergii* are suitable, especially purple varieties like 'Atropurpurea' and 'Atropurpurea Superba', which is more commonly found nowadays under its newer name of *B.* × *ottawensis* 'Purpurea', a larger and more spreading shrub. Other deciduous varieties worth considering are 'Buccaneer', which grows to about 5 feet (1.5 m) tall by about 4 feet (1.2 m) across and has

Berberis darwinii

Ground cover rose 'Grouse' (*top left*) beginning to cover a well mulched border

Rosa rugosa 'Roserie de l'Hai' (*top right*) – a first-rate taller ground cover rose

Ground cover rose 'Red Blanket' (*bottom*)

Late Dutch honeysuckle (*top right, overleaf*) will effectively cover a bank

Clematis 'William Kennett' (*top left, overleaf*) and *Clematis* 'Rouge Cardinale' (*bottom, overleaf*) can be pegged down to form ground cover

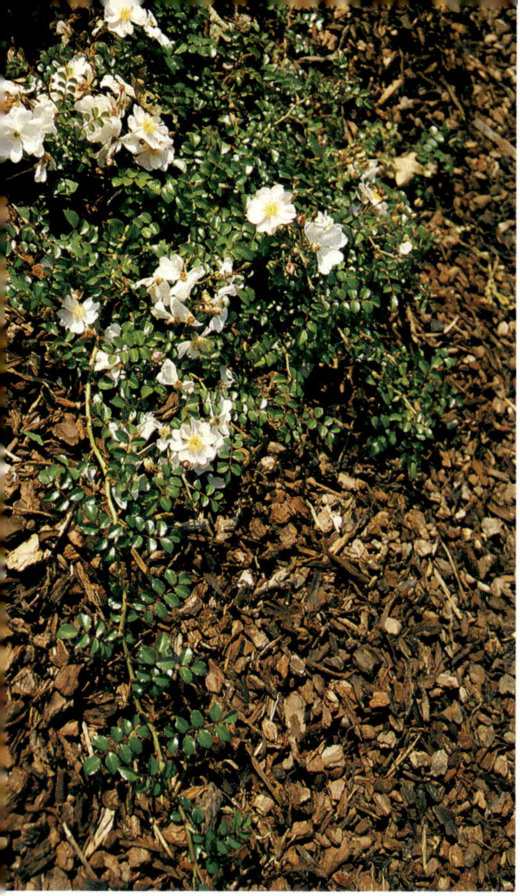

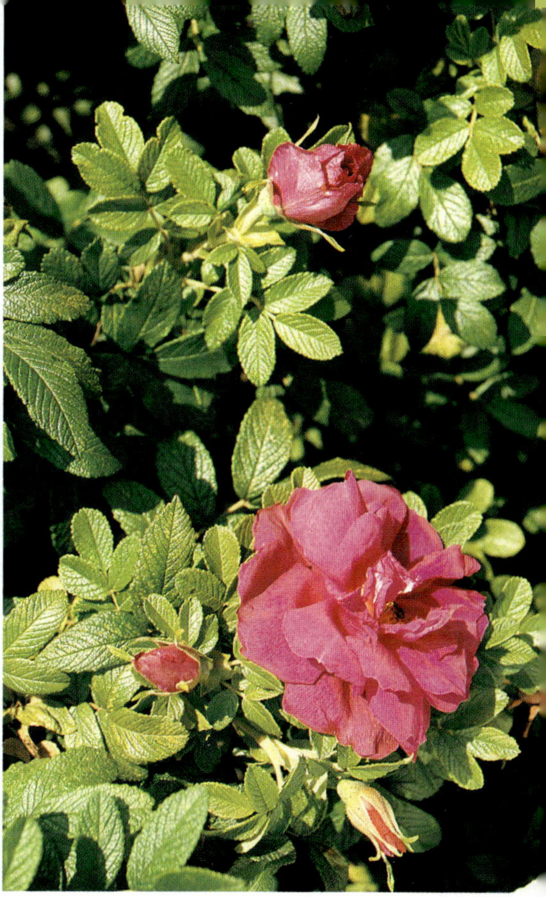

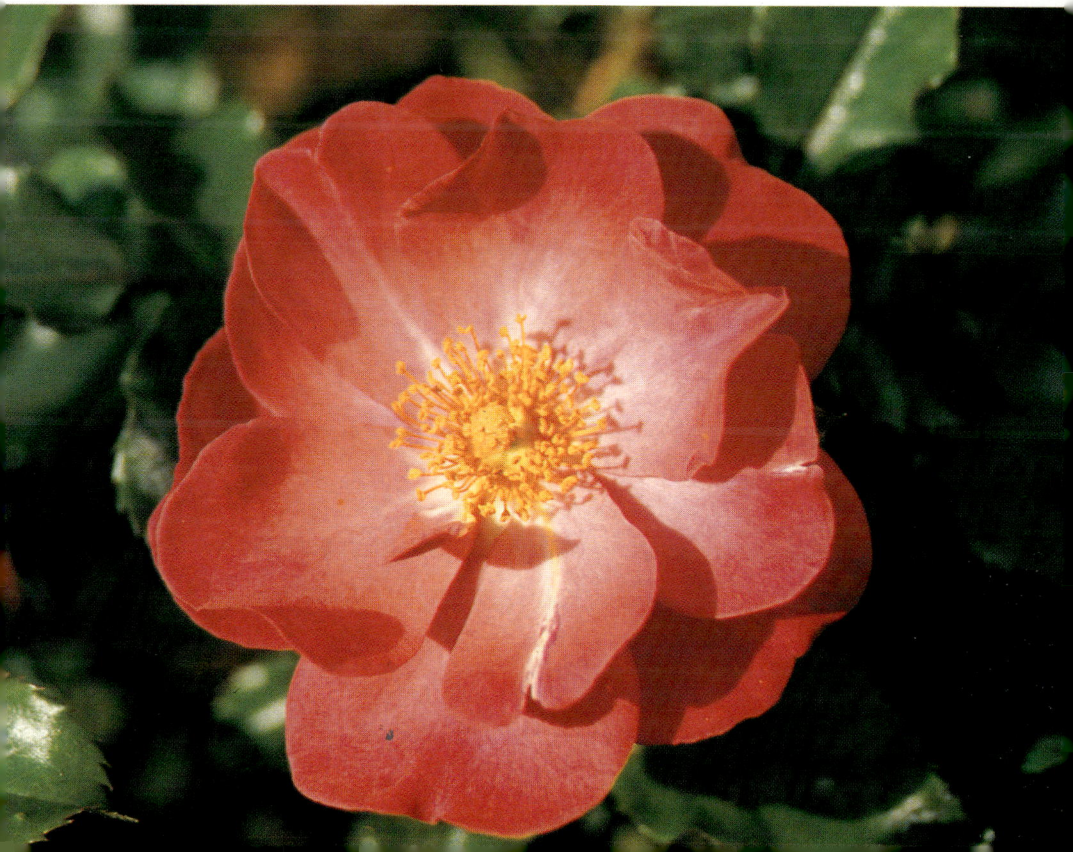

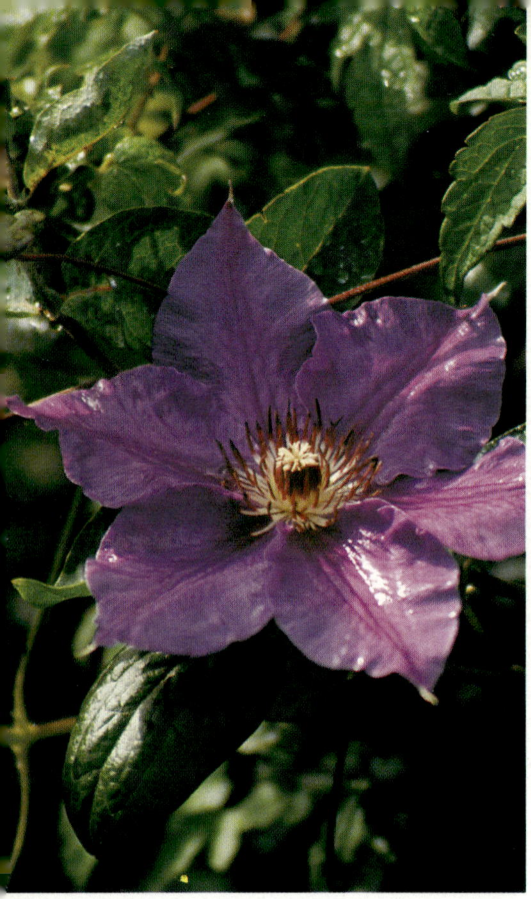
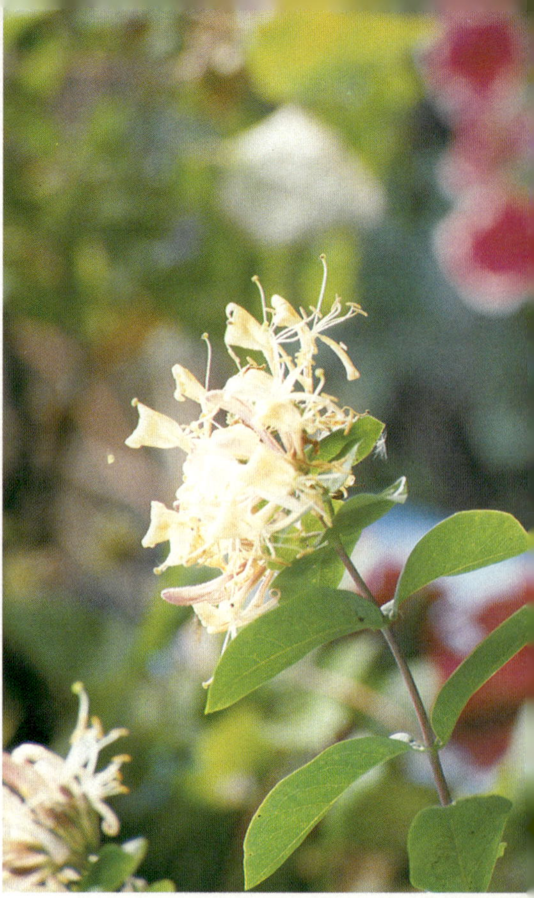
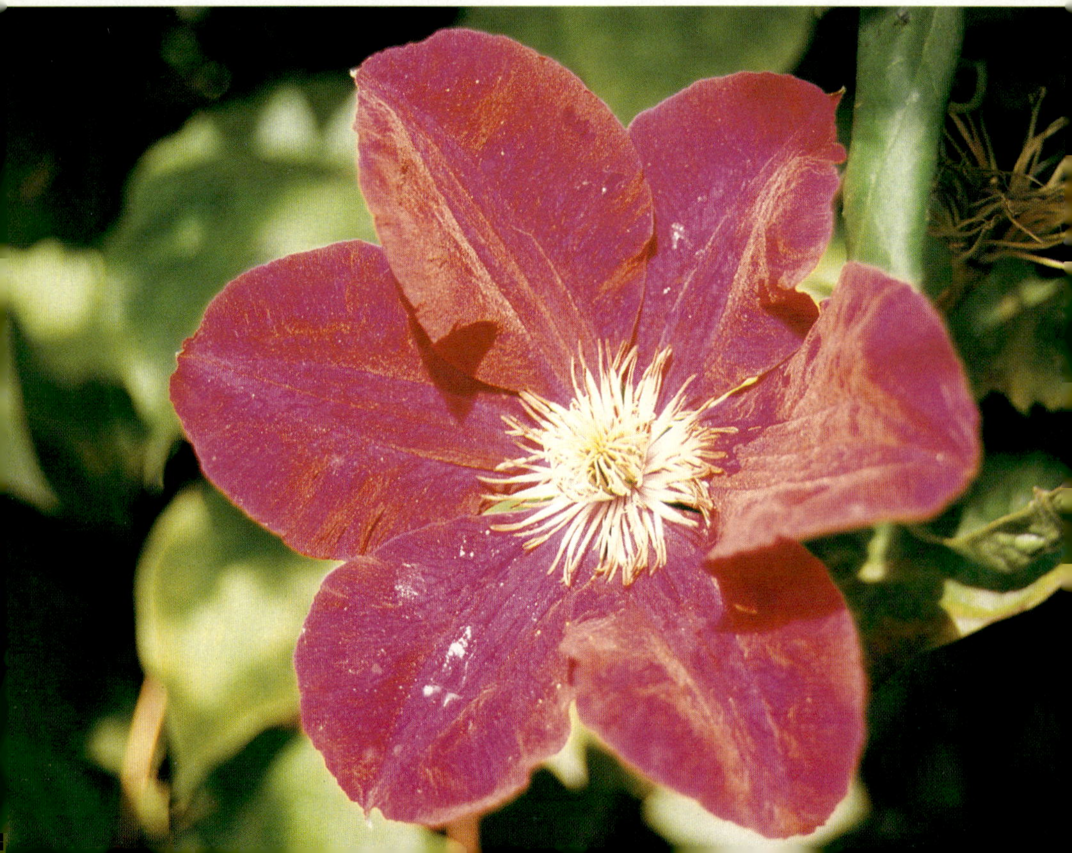

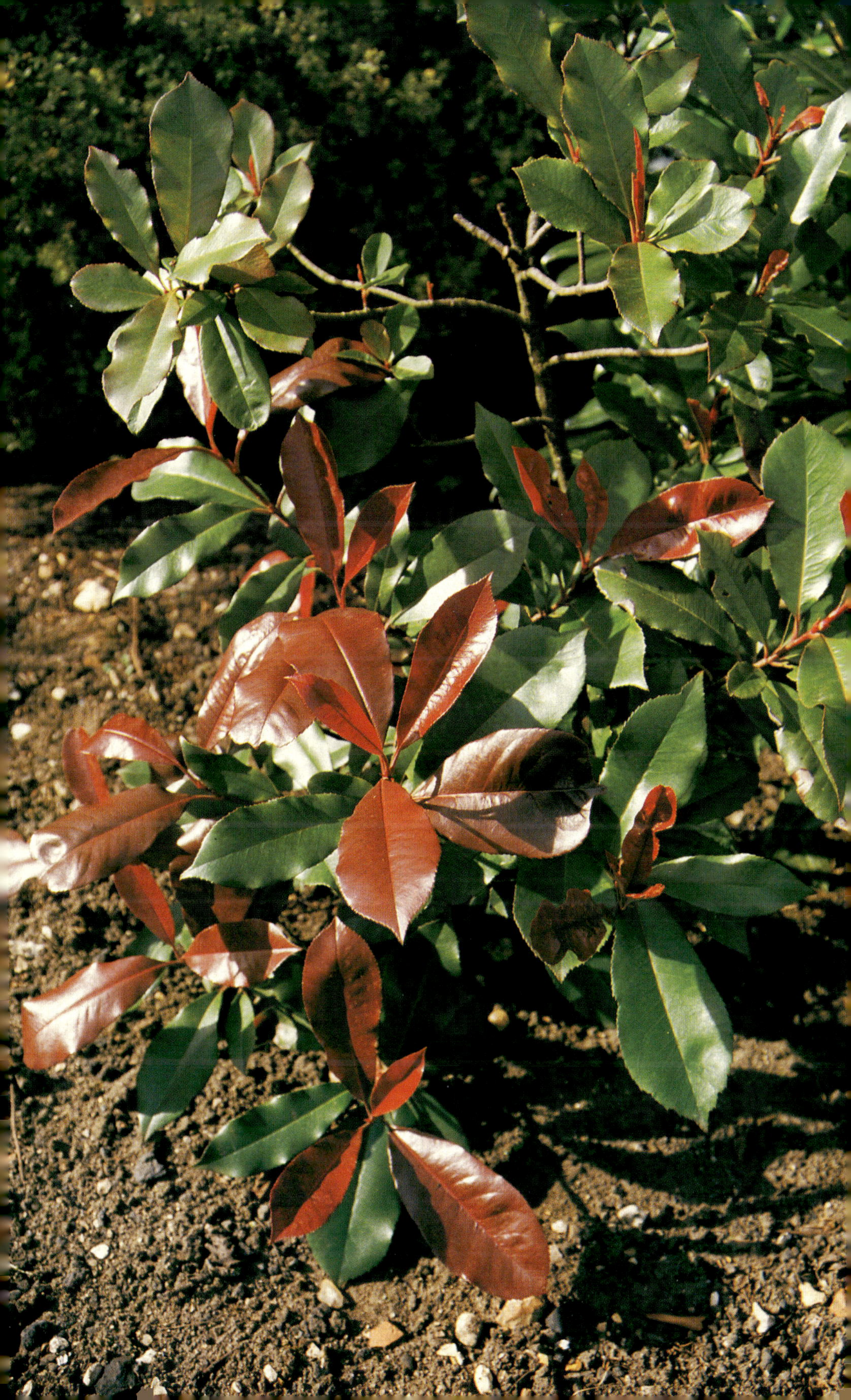

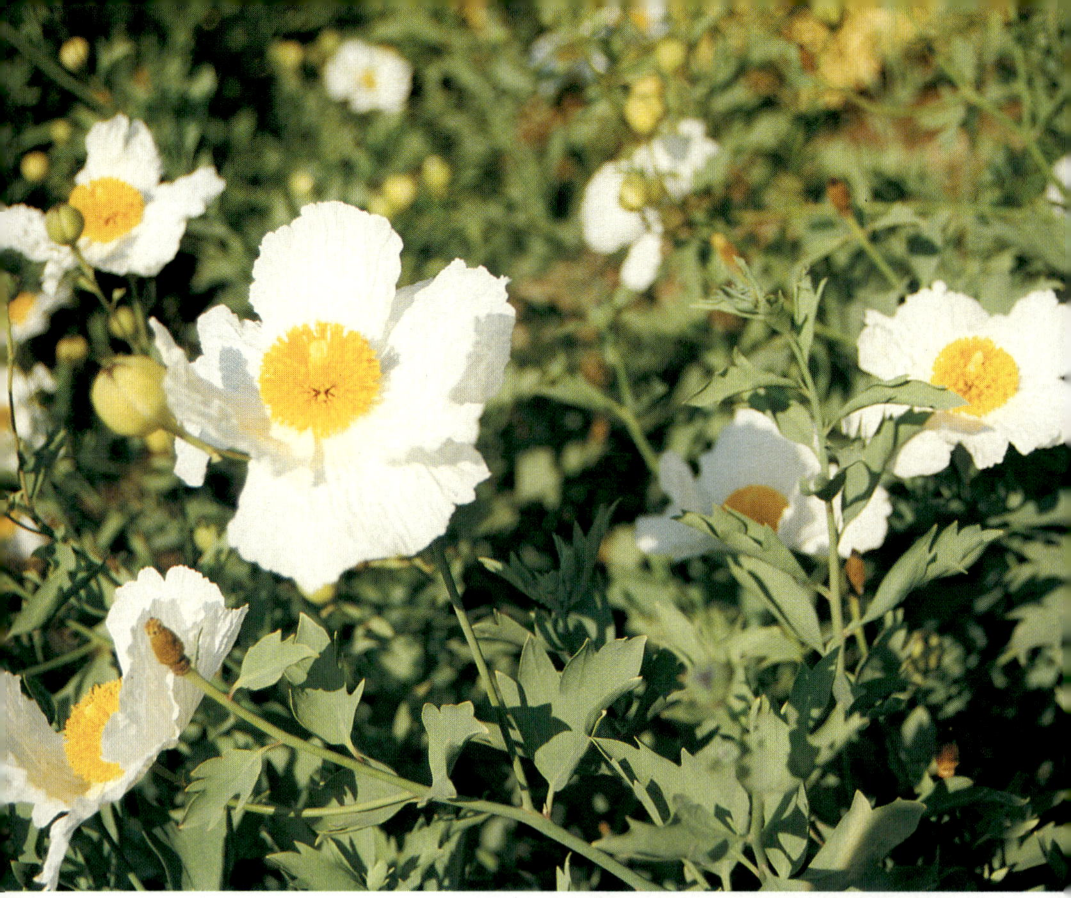
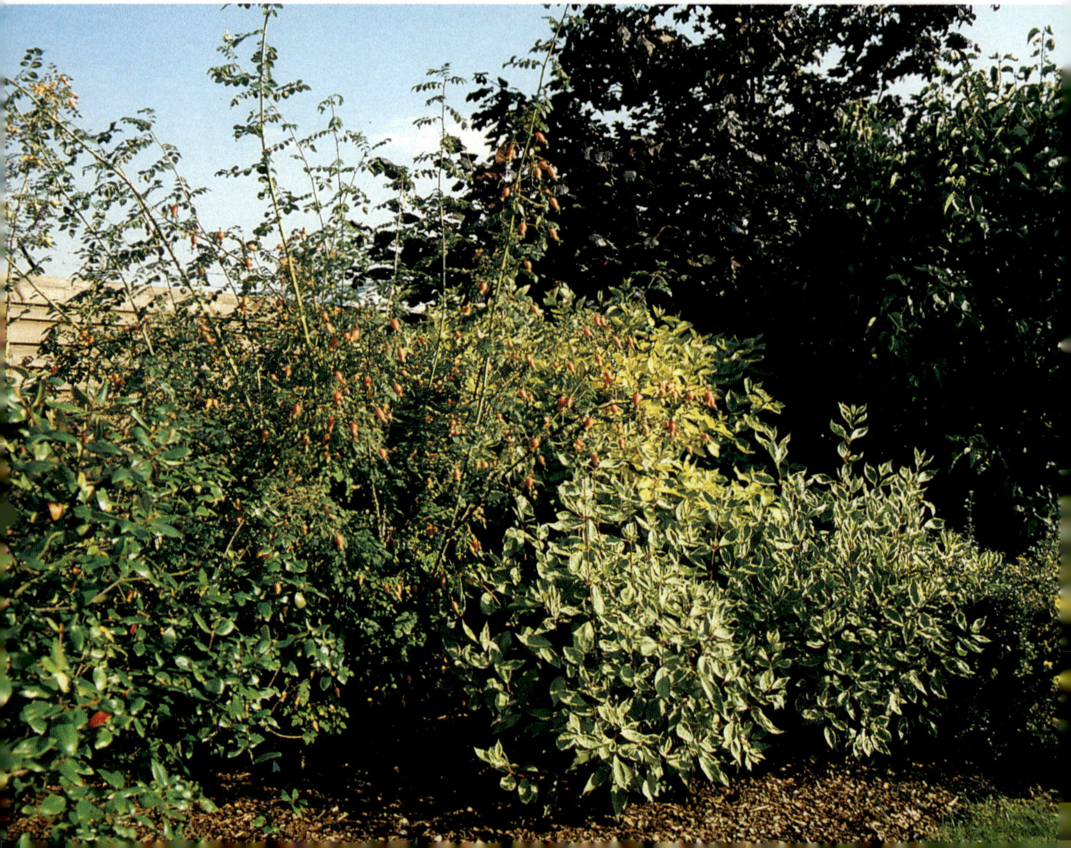

magnificent autumn colour, and *B. wilsonii,* a rounded bush 4 feet (1.2 m) tall and across, also with brilliant autumn colour, and a profusion of coral berries.

The best evergreen form for ground cover is possibly *B.* × *stenophylla,* which has a suckering, thicket-forming habit. The leaves are small and a very dark green, and the deep yellow spring flowers are scented. It is extremely thorny, and will make an impenetrable barrier in time. Its ultimate height is about 10 feet (3 m), although it can be clipped to keep it shorter, and each plant is capable of spreading more than 6 feet (2 m) across. A rather more restrained evergreen is *B. darwinii.* This has medium green leaves shaped rather like miniature holly leaves. It will eventually grow almost as tall as *B. stenophylla* and nearly as wide, but it does not sucker, and so is easier to keep in check. For the ultimate in vandal-proof cover, I would not hesitate to recommend *B. julianae;* its attractive red-tinted leaves, which are large for a berberis, being a bonus. Spacing for all berberis species is around 4 feet (1.2 m) apart.

Choisya ternata (Mexican orange blossom) is a rather up-market shrub for ground cover, but nonetheless a very effective one, although you do have to choose your spot, as frost damage can occur in severe winters. It has dark, evergreen, 'fingered' leaves which, when crushed, smell strongly of nutmeg. The yellow, daisy-like flowers are sweetly fragrant, appearing mainly in early summer but also at other times of the year. The shrub can be pruned back a little in June to encourage it to thicken up. In warmer parts of the country, each plant will eventually make a bush about 6 feet (2 m) tall by the same across. Plant at intervals of 3 feet (1 m) for rapid coverage, otherwise 4 feet (1.2 m) apart.

Many of the **dogwoods** make good taller cover if managed properly. *Cornus alba* is a fast-growing species with bright red stems which are a particular feature of the plant in winter after the leaves have fallen. It has many cultivars. 'Kesselringii' is less rampant and the stems are a purple-brown shade which blend well with lighter bark. *C. alba* 'Sibirica Albo-Variegata' and 'Elegantissima' are two cream-variegated forms which colour well in the autumn. Of the two,

---

Romneya hybrida **is a taller shrub that spreads by suckers**
Massed shrubs with bark mulch cut weeding to a minimum
Photinia **'Red Robin'** (*previous page*) – **a useful shrub where taller ground cover is required**

'Sibirica Albo-Variegata' is more compact. 'Spaethii' is similar in every detail to 'Elegantissima' except the variegations are gold. For really fast cover, the native *C. sanguinea* is useful, with stems of green flushed with red. As a contrast, it is a good idea to plant the yellow-barked *C. stolonifera* 'Flaviramea'. These varieties of cornus will spread better, especially when the plants are young, if they are 'stooled'; that is, cut back very hard, to the base or just above, every other spring. Space plants 3 feet (1 m) apart for quick cover, otherwise 4 feet (1.2 m) apart.

Corylus avellana, the native British hazel nut, is quite suitable for mass planting, the yellow catkins in very early spring and the edible nuts being the main attraction. Like cornus, this is another plant which is improved (as far as ground cover is concerned) by occasional 'stooling' or 'coppicing', but not as often as cornus, or the catkins and nuts will be lost. *C. avellana* spreads by suckering, and unchecked will reach about 10 feet (3 m) high by 6 feet (2 m) across in about six years. There is a more compact, golden form, 'Aurea', which looks well planted with the green, and also with the purple hazel nut, *C. maxima* 'Purpurea'. Spacing for corylus is at 4-foot (1.2–m) intervals.

Cotinus coggygria (smoke tree) grows about 10 feet (3 m) tall by 6 feet (2 m) wide, and has rounded leaves which turn bright shades of red and orange in autumn. The common name is derived from the bush's appearance in June and July, when it is covered with delicate-looking pink flowers which give the impression of it being covered with a thin wisp of smoke. The leaves of 'Atropurpurea' are slightly tinged with purple and the flowers are pale purple. The autumn colour is bright yellow. *C. coggygria* 'Notcutt's Variety' is the best purple-leaved form, with pink and purple inflorescences. Plant at intervals of 4 feet (1.2 m).

Some of the taller species of **cotoneaster** are very good as cover at the back of a border, but some have branches which are too open and widely spaced to provide really thorough weed control. Of the species which are suitable, *C. divaricus* is possibly the best as it is rapid-growing, dense, and with close, glossy leaves which colour well in the autumn before being shed. The berries are deep red. The habit is reasonably restrained, individual bushes being about 6 feet (2 m) tall by as far across, and should be spaced 3–4 feet (1–1.2 m) apart. *C. franchettii,* a semi-evergreen, has arching branches which soon make a good covering canopy. It is a taller shrub, reaching about 10 feet (3 m) in six to ten years, and has sage-coloured leaves with a white felt beneath. Many scarlet berries follow the abundance of white blossom. Space at intervals of 4–5 feet (1.2–1.5 m).

C. frigidus is a very large shrub which will turn into a small tree eventually, but it can be pruned back, which will both keep it in order and thicken it up. The large, long leaves have pinkish-red undersides in winter, and the berries are deep red. *C. frigidus* should be spaced 5 feet (1.5 m) apart. *C. lacteus* is an evergreen, dense of habit with semi-pendulous branches which form good cover. Again, it can grow very large if not controlled, but it is an attractive shrub and well worth planting. Initial spacing is at 5-foot (1.5–m) intervals. *C. rotundifolius,* a much smaller species, reaches about 3 feet (1 m) tall by slightly more across. It is dome-shaped and semi-evergreen and the leaves turn deep red in the autumn. These plants should be spaced at smaller intervals of 2½ feet (80 cm). *C. salicifolius floccosus* has long, flexible, arching branches and large, lanceolate, dark, shiny leaves which are fully evergreen except in hard winters. The red berries are borne in clusters. Spacing is at 4–foot (1.2–m) intervals.

Elaeagnus is another genus which includes many of the best ground-covering large shrubs. *Elaeagnus angustifolia* (oleaster), a large, deciduous shrub with many long spines, has willowy, silver-grey leaves and silvery-scaled young shoots. The flowers are fragrant and small, and are followed by berries of an unusual silvery-orange shade. Spacing for these is 5 feet (1.5 m) apart. *E. commutata* spreads by suckers and grows to about the same size as oleaster. It is also deciduous, the leaves being largish, narrowly ovate and silver in colour. The flowers are small and highly scented, appearing slightly earlier, in May, and are followed by greyish-silver fruit. The spacing is the same. *E.* × *ebbingei* also grows to about the same size, but it is an evergreen, having leathery, medium-sized leaves with silvery undersides. Very sweetly scented, insignificant-looking flowers appear in late autumn on the old wood. There are several very pleasing cultivars. 'Gilt Edge' is slower and ultimately makes a smaller bush, with leaves edged in gold. 'Limelight' is much larger and faster, with a bright yellow centre to the leaves. 'Gilt Edge' should be planted 3–4 feet (1–1.2 m) apart, the others 5 feet (1.5 m) apart. *E. macrophylla* is a very large, spreading, evergreen shrub, again with fragrant flowers in autumn. The young leaves are silvery, maturing green. Plant this species 5 feet (1.5 m) apart.

THE BIG COVER-UP

E. pungens 'Aureo-Maculata' and 'Variegata' are two similar evergreens with variegated leaves which start off slowly but eventually make quite big plants. They benefit from being pruned back to thicken them up. 'Aureo-Maculata' has a bright central splash of yellow; in 'Variegata' the green and yellow are reversed, and the yellow is rather paler. They have a tendency to revert to plain green; a close watch should be maintained and any all-green shoots removed entirely immediately as they are stronger-growing and can eventually take over the whole bush. Space at intervals of 4 feet (1.2 m). *E. umbellata parviflora* is a big, fast, thorny shrub with semi-evergreen, bright green leaves again having silvery underneaths. The flowers are small, white, fluffy and well-scented and appear in late spring and early summer. Plants should be spaced 5 feet (1.5 m) apart.

There are many species of **hydrangea** with a habit that makes them suitable for ground cover, but nothing can really surpass the well-known mopheads, forms of *Hydrangea macrophylla*, which have pink, red or blue heads according to the soil, blue being achieved in acid conditions. There are also one or two good whites, like 'Madame E. Moulliere'. Spacing is at 4-foot (1.2–m) intervals. For ground-cover purposes no regular pruning is necessary other than removing the old flower heads in spring, after they have remained to give protection to the flower buds for the following season throughout the winter. However, when the bushes are really mature, a proportion of the oldest branches can be removed at the base to encourage the production of young material. Some of the stronger-growing lacecaps, like 'Blue Wave', 'White Wave', 'Mariesii' (pink in alkaline

Hydrangea 'Blue Wave'

soil, blue in acid); 'Veitchii' (white outside, blue central florets), and 'Geoffrey Chadbund', which is a smaller form of a brick-red colour, are also suitable for mass planting.

As well as the cultivars, hydrangea species can make excellent cover. *H. paniculata* 'Grandiflora' is a large bush with heads of creamy-white flowers fading pink. The oak-leaved hydrangea, *H. quercifolia,* has large leaves resembling those of the oak which colour in autumn. The flowers are produced in late summer and early autumn and are white, maturing purplish. Of a similar size is *H.* 'Preziosa', which has young leaves and stems of an unusual brownish-red colour. The flowers are similar to the 'mop-heads' but smaller, salmon-pink in colour when they open, but turning red. Spacing for the mop-heads and lacecaps is 4 feet (1.2 m) apart, for larger species such as *H. paniculata* 'Grandiflora' 4–5 feet (1.2–1.5 m) apart, and for smaller species 2½–3 feet (80 cm-1 m) apart.

Hippophae rhamnoides (sea buckthorn) is a familiar sight on our sand-dunes, especially on the east coast, but should not be discounted as a ground-cover shrub as it makes useful, low-maintenance spread. It grows into a big shrub in time, but can be clipped to keep it more manageable. The leaves are willow-like and grey, and the female plants produce bright orange berries. It is extremely thorny, and is therefore useful for areas liable to be vandalized, and because it can withstand a high degree of salt, both as spray and in the soil, it is handy for gardens bordering main roads which are salted in winter or those which receive salt-laden gales. Plants should be spaced 4 feet (1.2 m) apart.

Not all species of **ilex** (holly) make good ground cover as they can be rather slow and the growth habit is often too upright to look right. The common holly, *Ilex aquifolium* is one of the best for this purpose, as it has a fairly dense form and the canopy prevents most light from reaching the ground, while the dead leaves make a barrier underneath which deters both weed seedlings and slugs! A big plantation of common holly can look rather dreary, though, even when it includes some good berrying female plants, but the silver holly, *I. aquifolium* 'Argentea Marginata' is similar except for the colour of the leaves, which are broadly margined in silver. The silver holly also has male and female forms, and it is essential to get a proportion of each if you want berries. Spacing again depends on the speed at which you want the space filled up, but should start at 3-foot (1–m) intervals,

THE BIG COVER-UP

although for economy the plants can be positioned further apart.

I have recommended one form of the **mahonia** genus, *Mahonia aquifolium,* for binding loose earth, but there are many others which are more attractive, with yellow, lily-of-the-valley shaped and scented flowers, which provide good coverage when planted close together. The most widely planted is *M. japonica,* sometimes wrongly referred to as *M. bealii,* which has long, leathery, pinnate leaves in rosettes. The flowers appear very early, sometimes in November, and remain on the bushes until well into the new year. It tends to be a rather narrow shrub but it can be encouraged to bush out by being cut back after flowering – it will stand quite hard pruning. *M.* × 'Charity' is similar, but the flowers usually appear later in the winter. *M. pinnata* is shorter, with sea-green leaves, and it flowers in March. *M.* 'Undulata' is thought to be a hybrid between this and *M. aquifolium,* and grows to nearly 6 feet (2 m) high, with wavy, dark green leaves and bright yellow flower spikes in spring. Spacing for *M. pinnata* is 3 feet (1 m) apart, and for all the others 4 feet (1.2 m) apart.

Pyracantha (firethorn) are generally thought of as wall shrubs, but they do, in fact, make really good free-standing bushes and,

Firethorn in flower

planted closely enough together, are ideal ground-cover plants. All pyracanthas are evergreen (although in really bad winters many of the older leaves are inclined to fall off) and have white flowers in early summer which are rather like may blossom in form and scent, followed by bright berries. There are many varieties readily available from garden centres these days, most of which are resistant to the scab disease which was such a disfiguring drawback to some of the older forms.

P. angustifolia prefers a warm site, as it can sometimes be damaged during the winter. It has quite small, narrow leaves which have a white felt on the undersides and in good seasons produces an enormous crop of orange-yellow berries. 'Mojave' has bright red berries and is a strong and trouble-free cultivar, showing some resistance even to fireblight disease which has become in recent time the scourge of many members of the family Rosaceae. It is a serious, often fatal, disease and shows itself in the sudden collapse of all or part of the bush, which looks as though a bonfire has been lit too near to it and has scorched all the foliage. Sometimes the shrub will recover if the affected parts are completely removed, but not always. Until recently the Ministry of Agriculture had to be notified if the disease appeared, but it became so widespread in certain years that it was impossible to deal with all the cases, and so it is not notifiable any longer. If you know there have been incidences of fireblight in your locality, you may be wise to steer clear of pyracantha on a large scale, unless you stick to 'Mojave'.

'Orange Glow' is an old favourite which has a very dense habit and large orange-red berries. *P. rogersiana* makes a well-branched shrub with bright red berries. It also has a yellow-berried form, 'Flava', and a mixture of the two sorts looks good in a massed planting. 'Soleil d'Or' is particularly useful for covering ground as it is very lax and spreading. It also has yellow berries, which are larger than those of 'Flava', and comparatively large, green leaves. It has tremendous powers of rejuvenation if cut hard back once established, and if the planting starts to look rather open, a good pruning will thicken it up. 'Wateri' is one of the best red-berried forms, and also grows quickly to form an impenetrable thicket. Spacing for most varieties of pyracantha is from 4 feet (1.2 m) apart depending on your patience (or lack of it).

Photinia is a very attractive shrub which could cost you a bob or two to use as ground cover because individual plants are not cheap, but you might feel the eventual effect to be worth it. The most commonly sold form is *Photinia* × *fraseri* 'Red Robin', which has largish, oval leaves coloured an amazing bright red when they first appear, gradually turning green. 'Red Robin' should be given a sheltered, warm position to prevent frost damage. Left unpruned, it will reach a height of about 6 feet (2 m) in time, but without a little attention the habit is somewhat sparse and straggly. Cutting the young branches back by about half will help to thicken it up, and also induces the best overall colour as it produces many young shoots from the remaining leaf buds. If this is done during the summer when the first flush of new leaves has started to turn bronze it will ensure the plants retain their red colour for an extended period.

Similar to *P.* × *fraseri* 'Red Robin' in many respects, and also similar to cotoneaster, as it is a close relative of both, is **stranvaesia**. *Stranvaesia davidiana* is a large, evergreen or semi-evergreen shrub with long, narrow leaves, white flowers rather like pyracantha, and red berries. It too, has red-coloured young leaves, which help to give a mass planting an interesting look. *S. davidiana* 'Palette' is a variegated cultivar which is a bit special, the new shoots appearing bright pink, and maturing to shades of green, white, cream and even reddish tints. It is another slightly pricey shrub so I do not recommend it for large areas, but a small group in a sunny, well-drained, warm spot looks really smart. Plant *Photinia* × *fraseri* 'Red Robin' 3–4 feet (1–1.2 m) apart, *Stranvaesia davidiana* at intervals of 4–5 feet (1.2–1.5 m), and *S. d.* 'Palette' at 4- foot (1.2–m) intervals.

The widely recognized **common laurel** *(Prunus laurocerasus)* makes excellent cover as the large, thick, leathery leaves exclude all light from the ground beneath and the dead leaves, if not cleared up, lie as a waterproof mulch. Common laurel can be pruned back with secateurs (preferably not trimmed with shears, which make the plants look unsightly as the leaves which have been cut in half usually turn brown and drop off) to virtually any height. Portugal laurel is nearly as good, as it has a dense habit although the leaves are smaller. It has a bonus of white, tassel-like flowers in early summer, followed by purple, poisonous (to humans, but not to birds) cherry-like fruit. There is a nicely variegated form which appears to advantage when planted in bold groups. Plants should be spaced 4 feet (1.2 m) apart or less.

TALLER SHRUBS AS GROUND COVER

Romneya hybrida (Californian poppy) is a very pretty sub-shrub with long, erect, suckering stems up to about 5 feet (1.5 m) tall. The stems are bluish-green, as are the leaves, which are poppy-shaped. Fragrant white flowers with deep yellow stamens are produced on top of the stems between July and September. Each plant will cover a great deal of space in time, but it can take a year or two to get started, and so I would recommend spacing the plants about 3 feet (1 m) apart initially. *R. hybrida* is quicker off the mark in light soil.

I have mentioned the various low-growing forms of **Rosa rugosa** in the chapter on ground-cover roses (see pages 103–112), but I purposely omitted *R. rugosa* itself because, although it is a very good covering plant, it is not ideal for every garden as it is quite large, reaching over 6 feet (2 m) if unpruned, and spreads widely by means of suckers, so I felt it fitted more comfortably into this section of the book.

R. rugosa is usually bought in seedling form as it germinates very well and comes true to type. As a result you are likely to get a variety of colours, mainly magenta, but with some paler mauve ones and some white flowered plants as well. It has a very pleasant perfume and flowers continuously from early summer until autumn, and when the flowers fade they are followed by large, red, globular hips. The stems are a mass of thorns, which look fine but are really quite beastly, so *R. rugosa* is useful for areas at risk from vandalism. The foliage in autumn turns a bright yellow before dropping. Regular pruning is unnecessary, but after a while you may find the appearance of the group is improved by cutting out the very old wood. Initial spacing is about 2 feet (60 cm), although the plants can be positioned much further apart and will still join to give good coverage.

Sambucus (elder) will have many people throwing up their hands in horror, but the fact is that the common elder, *Sambucus nigra,* has many attractive coloured-leaved forms which are ideal for mass planting; for example, the golden elder, *S. nigra* 'Aurea', variegated cultivars such as the cream-margined 'Albo-variegata' and gold-margined 'Aurea-marginata', and the purple tinted 'Purpurea'; all of which have snowy white flower heads and edible berries just like the native of the hedgerows. These all grow quite big, but the golden cut-leaved elder, *S. racemosa* 'Plumosa Aurea' is a much more restrained shrub. This will never grow too large if it is cut back periodically to produce the young wood, which always bears the brightest coloured leaves. Space *S. nigra* varieties 4–6 feet (1.2–2 m) apart and *S. racemosa* 'Plumosa Aurea' 4 feet (1.2 m) apart.

The best forms of **willow** to use for taller ground cover are those with coloured bark, and these look particularly good when used in conjunction with cornus alba varieties and the ornamental brambles, rubus, with 'whitewashed' stems (for example *R. cockburnianus* and *R. thibetanus*). Those willows with the brightest stems are *Salix alba* 'Vitellina' (yellow), 'Chermesina' (orange-scarlet), *S. daphnoides* (deep purple with a white bloom), *S. fargesii* (reddish-brown), *S. purpurea* (purple tinted), and 'Sekka', which has purplish-brown stems that can be curiously fasciated and contorted and so are popular with flower arrangers. As the brightest colour is found on the newest growth, it is a wise move to cut all willows grown for their bark down to ground level in spring, and this will keep them at a reasonable height. A mass planting of those species which have showy catkins, such as *S. caprea* (pussy or goat willow) and *S. medemii* are also attractive. Spacing for these species of willow and also for the varieties of rubus mentioned is around 4 feet (1.2 m).

The common **snowberry**, *Symphoricarpos albus* 'Laevigatus', can become a nuisance in many gardens as it spreads rapidly by means of suckers which often come up quite a distance from the parent plant. It does, however, suppress weeds very well and both when the bushes

Symphoricarpos 'Mother of Pearl'

are covered with pink flowers and later when the branches are laden with white berries it can look very presentable. Most forms of snowberry produce suckers, but one group, the S. *doorenbosii* hybrids, which include 'Magic Berry' (carmine berries), 'Mother of Pearl' (berries tinted pink), and 'White Hedge', do not sucker and are much more compact plants, which makes them ideal for modern plantings. Spacing for suckering forms is 3 feet (1 m) apart, for non-suckering varieties at 2-foot (60–cm) intervals.

While on the subject of suckering shrubs, **Spiraea × billardii 'Triumphans'** is another which will rapidly fill a lot of space for very little outlay. As a specimen it is a nightmare – the stems come up all over the place where you do not want them to – but in a single planting it can look quite pretty. It flowers all summer with fluffy heads of a medium pink and in certain seasons the leaves turn yellow before they fall. Space plants 3 feet (1 m) or more apart.

There are several species of **viburnum,** both evergreen and deciduous, which can be used for filling large areas with a single variety. *Viburnum tinus* is perhaps the most suitable evergreen as it is dense and fast-growing, thriving in nearly every circumstance with the exception of very low temperatures, when some die-back can occur. The pink flower buds start to appear in autumn, opening to flat white heads in winter and early spring. No pruning is necessary, but if you should want to reduce the size of the bushes, they usually can be trimmed back immediately after flowering without having an adverse effect on the following season's blooms.

The other evergreen viburnum which covers well and suppresses weeds is *V. rhytidophyllum,* a tall, rapid-growing shrub with large, dark, deeply veined leaves with white felt on their undersides and heads of dirty white flowers in June followed by red berries which eventually turn black. The two best deciduous species are both British natives. The first is the wayfaring tree, *V. lantana,* which is a tall shrub with ribbed, slightly furry leaves, white flowers in late spring, then red berries turning black. The second is the guelder rose, *V. opulus,* which is as useful for its bright autumn leaves as for its white flower heads and red berries. It has a yellow-berried form – *V. o.* 'Fructo-Luteo' and there is a non-berrying variety with big white sterile flower heads known as *V. o.* 'Sterile' and is also often referred to as the Japanese snowball tree. Spacing for all species is 3–4 feet (1–1.2 m) apart.

The common gorse, **Ulex europaeus,** is another useful species where vandalism is likely to occur, as it is extremely unpleasant to handle. The bushes will reach about 6 feet (2 m) in height by about 5 feet (1.5 m) wide given time, and although the main flush of flowers is in the spring, the bushes are seldom seen without some yellow, pea-like blooms on them. The double-flowered form 'Plenus' is slightly smaller and more compact; the foliage on the bushes is almost completely hidden by the semi-double yellow blossom in April and May. Plants should be spaced 3 feet (1 m) apart.

This is my choice of larger shrubs suitable for ground cover, but it was difficult deciding which to include and which should be omitted as there are so many which would fit the bill merely by planting large quantities close together. For instance, one of the most magnificent sights I have ever seen was a large space completely filled with forsythia, but I have purposely left this out, along with others of a similar nature, because for too long in the year they do not do much other than look green or brown, but I have to admit that if they were used with other more exciting material they would be perfectly acceptable as ground-cover shrubs. If you are thinking about planting up areas for ground cover, the ideas in this book are not the only things you can do. Use your imagination and, if you can visualize living with a mass of anything you fancy, then go ahead and use it. Provided you plant closely enough to cut maintenance to a minimum, it is more than possible that what you choose to plant will work for you very well.

Useful addresses and Bibliography

Nurseries
Notcutt's Nurseries, Woodbridge, Suffolk: Wide range of all types of plants. Also have garden centres at Nuneham Courtney, Bagshot, Maidstone, St Albans, Peterborough, Ardleigh, Norwich, and Solihull, where postal orders may be collected.

Bressingham Gardens, Diss, Norfolk: specialists in alpines, dwarf conifers, shrubs for modern gardens, heathers and herbaceous plants for collection at the plant centre or by mail order.

Hillier Nurseries (Winchester), Ltd, Ampfield House, Ampfield, Romsey, Hampshire: very wide range of all types of plants including many unusual varieties. Hillier Garden Centres at Southampton, Horsham, Liss, Romsey, Sunningdale, Winchester, Ampfield.

Crowders Nurseries, Lincoln Road, Horncastle, Lincs, LN9 5ZL.

Roses as ground cover are well displayed in many nurseries, for example, at David Austin Roses, Bowling Green Lane, Albrighton, Wolverhampton, West Midlands.

Specialist clubs and organizations
British Pteridological (Fern) Society, 42 Lewisham Road, Smethwick, Warley, West Midlands.

Hardy Plant Society, 10 St Barnabas Road, Emmer Green, Caversham, Reading, Berks.

British Hosta and Hemerocallis Society, 42 Fairoak Drive, Eltham, London SE9.

The Royal National Rose Society, Chiswell Green, St Albans, Herts, should also be helpful on the subject of roses as ground cover.

Suggested further reading
Guide to the Specialist Nurseries and Garden Suppliers of Britain and Ireland, edited by Sarah Cotton, Garden Art Press.
The Dry Garden, Beth Chatto, Dent.
The Damp Garden, Beth Chatto, Dent.
Hillier's Manual of Trees and Shrubs, David and Charles.
The Flower Expert, Dr D Hessayon, pbi Publications.
Plants for Shade, Allen Paterson, Dent.
Plants for Small Gardens, Geoffrey K Coombes, Cassells (Wisley Handbook Series).
Fisk's Clematis Nursery Catalogue, 65p, including postage, from Fisk's Clematis Nursery, Westleton, Saxmundham, Suffolk. A comprehensive booklet dealing with planting, training, maintenance and problems of clematis, with a list of most of the species and varieties available at present, well illustrated with colour photographs.
Clematis, Ethne Rouss Clarke, Collins Aura Handbooks.
The Hardy Plant Society's New Plant Directory, Chris Phillip, Moorland Publishing.

Useful Pieces of Equipment
Some excellent hose-end attachments are made by Gardena Systems. Hobby shears, for cutting thick wire for example, are obtainable from Wolf Tools of Ross-on-Wye, Hereford and Worcester.